About the Author

Andrew Sweeney always had a passion for writing and reading anything he could get his hands on. Also, delving into the human psyche and trying to understand the reasons for our different behaviours, is something of major interest to him. He hopes that comes across in what you're about to read. If it can help you in some way, on the journey we know as life, that would give him the greatest satisfaction, from a professional point of view.

The Minority

Andrew Sweeney

The Minority

Olympia Publishers
London

www.olympiapublishers.com
OLYMPIA PAPERBACK EDITION

A CIP catalogue record for this title is
available from the British Library.

ISBN: 978-1-80439-207-2

This is a work of fiction.
Names, characters, places and incidents originate from the writer's
imagination. Any resemblance to actual persons, living or dead, is
purely coincidental.

First Published in 2023

Olympia Publishers
Tallis House
2 Tallis Street
London
EC4Y 0AB

Printed in Great Britain

Dedication

I would like to dedicate this book to departed family and friends, who are always in our hearts.

Acknowledgements

Thank you to all family, friends and colleagues, who have stood by me on my journey so far. This is just the beginning and the most wonderful happiness is yet to come.

Prologue

The grass of the field whistled in the wind of the early evening sun. The boy had been here many times before to explore and make up fantasies of his own worlds and civilisations. Today, he was the leader of a Celtic tribe, trying to ward off an invasion from the Roman Empire. He armed himself with a large stick, he had discovered whilst walking and brandished it in his right hand. He marched up the grassy hill to face the enemy which lay in wait, on the other side. Carefully, he ascended as he neared the top, as not to give any indication to his enemy that he was there. He had concluded that the element of surprise would be the best course of action in this instance.

He charged down the other side of the hill so carefully. As to not get any mud or grass stains on his person, as that was the last thing he wanted to happen. He knew from past experiences that would spoil everything later. He would not be able to enjoy his victory, when in the comfort of his own bed, replaying the day's events through his mind.

The boy slashed at his enemies and pivoted to block their attacks upon him. One by one he cut through them or charged them down, shouting in his head "You will not take our land!" He silently repeated this over and over as he bobbed, weaved, slashed, and tore at the unspeakable threat to his people.

With the battle won and victory secured. He reascended the hill from which he had come down and sat upon a big log that lay across the grass on the top. From there he could see for miles around in every direction. The boy decided that this was the place a leader of a tribe such as his, should sit. Here, he felt like the ruler of the world. Though, he decided that he wasn't interested in the rest of the world. Only in looking after his tribe and making sure no harm came to them. From the Romans or anybody else who would try to take their land away from them.

He carefully checked his clothing and whole body for any stains, as he knew that would be disastrous. Satisfied that there were none, he took out of his pocket the small packet of fudge he had bought from Raymond's shop, that stood around the corner from his actual home, on the way here. Fudge was his favourite treat, and he would procure it whenever he could.

As he sat on the log enjoying his fudge, he looked around him and as he did, he concluded that this here was the best place on Earth. This was his place and he never wanted anybody to discover it and take it from him. He thought it important not to tell anybody of this place. That way, he could come here every day after school, protect his tribe from invaders and eat his fudge, if he had any. The last thing he wanted was for any of the other boys at school to catch him here or spot him on the way and follow him. He decided that every time he came back here, he would come by a different route and if he felt like he was being followed, abandon the plan to come here and go somewhere else. He must protect his tribe at all costs, and nobody must know of this place. For here, he was safe, happy, and secure with his tribe. The sound of the local church bells ringing suddenly broke his train of thought.

"Oh, no!" he screamed out loud. "That is the 7 o'clock strike! I must have lost track of the time. I'm going to be late home and he will not be pleased."

The boy quickly descended the hill again, silently praying

that he didn't splash any mud onto himself. He made it through the fields and ran through the streets to his home. When walking, this would have taken around five minutes. Through his haste he made it within two.

There he stood at the front door to the house when the boy arrived. Sheepishly, the boy approached him with his head bowed. All he could hope is that he hadn't noticed what time it was. The boy admonished himself in his head for being so stupid, getting so caught up in his games that he forgot what time it was. Punctuality was of major importance to him, and the boy knew it.

"What time were you supposed to be back here?" The man asked with an unnerving, calm authority.

"7pm." The boy nervously answered.

"Well, it is past 7pm now, isn't it?" he asked rhetorically.

"I never meant to be late, honest I didn't!" the boy pleaded. "I just got lost in my thoughts when I was walking, that's all. I ran back here as fast as I could when I heard the church bells ring," he stammered.

"It's okay," the man calmly said. As the boy approached, he put his arm on his shoulder and spoke, "Let us just hope you're not a dirty boy, as well as a late boy."

Chapter 1

"This is one of my favourite tunes!" Mikey exuded to Rachel as 'Arabella' by the Arctic Monkeys played on the workplace radio.

Mikey Wainwright. A man in his late twenties, of below average height and somewhat skinny for a socially acceptable male appearance. His wonderfully thick black hair, ocean blue eyes and strong jawline, more than made up for any perceived shortcomings and gave him a relatively attractive appearance. Though Mikey would often examine himself in the mirror when alone in his one bedroomed, above shop, apartment in the town of Bury, Greater Manchester. Situated in the north west of England. A town famous for its market and black pudding produce. He sometimes stared for long periods, dreaming up ways of how he could improve his appearance. His name had also proved problematic in the past, as it is not short for Michael, as people he had encountered assumed.

"What is it with that?" Mikey would often think. "What was the thinking behind such a stupid name?"

He always knew that when his train of thought went down this path, he had to pull himself off it, as that led to thinking about the bad thing and that was to be avoided at all costs.

"We all have our favourites," Rachel answered. Not bothering to look up from her phone screen. Rachel, with her flowing, long, dark hair, near six-foot height, size twelve figure, and Hollywood smile, aligned with her striking beauty, would normally make for an intimidating presence for a guy like Mikey, whose shyness and insecurities about his appearance, made it difficult for him to communicate effectively in conversations. Especially with a beauty like Rachel. Though, as Mikey and Rachel had been working colleagues for the past eighteen months at Energy Records, a music shop with its own small recording label, based on The Rock in the centre of the town, made him somewhat more comfortable in talking to her.

Mikey's role at the shop was working in the back. Sorting online orders and packaging orders for the customers who came into the shop. He very rarely dealt with customers on the shop floor and on the occasions this was unavoidable, he instantly felt the sweat escape from his pores and run down his back. He had to focus hard to not let his body shake from the excruciating fear.

Rachel is the colleague that he spends the most time with, as she mainly works on the administration side of things in the back with him. He felt he had built up a certain rapport and working relationship with her. Something that did make him smile when he thought about it. Even though she sometimes became angry with him when she felt his work wasn't up to scratch. Or chastised him for being lazy, or 'work shy', as she put it. He had noticed she would always do this when she herself had been idle and seemingly not much work on. He thought she must have been working hard and wanted a rest. So, he would on these occasions, talk to himself and try to drum a better work ethic into his day. Even though he did seem to be busy for most of his days and had very little time for breaks. Even lunch was on the go most days. He concluded that Rachel must just be so much more competent and efficient than him, as she always had ample time for breaks. He strived to be better.

"Have you managed to arrange the sticker collection of old rock classics that Mr Jefferson requested as yet, Rachel?"

Siobhan asked with the affection and courtesy she always had when addressing her.

"Yes, of course. I did it this morning," Rachel replied handing over the book from her desk. Mr Jefferson had become a valued customer of Energy Records in the last six months or so. He is the old rocker type, with long greying hair who collected vinyl and stickers of his favourite bands. Mikey had noticed whenever he was in the shop, he would wave at him from the counter when he was sitting at his desk. The door to the back was always open, as to make for easy communication back and forth when needed. He always seemed to want to be friendly to Mikey and although these communication attempts made him feel nervous, he knew he felt a connection to them also. Such as, on a rare occasion, Mikey was near the front counter, he had told him about how he had managed to retire early after accepting a redundancy and pension package from the car plant he had worked at for over thirty years. Now, he delighted in the fact that he had more time for his hobbies, such as collecting vinyl. He seemed to take an interest in Mikey and always made sure he wished him well before leaving the shop. Mikey saw him as a warm and friendly guy. He also knew he appreciated his warmth.

"Fabulous, my special girl!" exclaimed Siobhan, who was the manager at the shop and answered only to Sean Meltzer, the store owner and label boss.

Rachel smiled and blushed before turning her attention back to the laptop on her desk. Though Rachel's primary role was working in the back with Mikey, she was more than willing to help at the front desk when needed. Especially, when there was a bit of 'eye-candy' that needed her attention. He had seen her go there even when there were no customers in the store and talk to either Tariq, or Beth, or both if they happened to be there together, as they were the two responsible for running the front of the shop. He thought they must have very important business to discuss during these times. He knew at these moments he was solely responsible for the office area. So, he endeavoured to plough through the work and try not to make a mistake. He knew Siobhan hated mistakes. He had found this out to his displeasure on many occasions.

Mikey had expected Rachel to mention to Siobhan that he had helped with the sticker book for Mr Jefferson; however, she hadn't. Which he thought was strange. Siobhan approached his desk, which diverted his thoughts back into the room.

She approached, tossing her auburn hair back as she did. Mikey always thought she looked well for her age, considering she was by now in her late fifties. She must have looked after herself over the years.

"Did you see Spark Town perform on TV last night? Oh, they were fabulous. Don't you think?" She warmly glowed to Mikey, standing in front of his desk. Spark Town are a local group who were spotted playing in a local pub by Sean Meltzer and signed to Energy Records. By now, they had made it onto the national stage and had been snapped up by a major label. Siobhan delighted in the fact that she had played an important role in furthering their career and would tell anybody that would listen, about how she helped make them the superstars they are today. She knew that Mikey was a big fan and so, loved to talk with him about them whenever the opportunity arose.

"Yes, I watched it," Mikey replied, frantically trying to think of something additional to say. He was after all, speaking to his manager and he desperately wanted to appear as though he had some semblance of intelligence about him. "I thought they were very good," he eventually managed. "Though, I think it will take a little time for the new bass player to settle in. Some of their bass lines are quite intricate and it will take a little time before he is fully up to speed with them and can blend in nicely with the rest of the band. He clearly has talent. Though, the chemistry is not quite there yet between him and the rest of the group. I feel as though it will come, the more they play together. It was such a shame what happened to Tony, with all his problems," Mikey replied. His mind working overtime to make sure his words were correct. Tony was the original bass player of the band, though had left because of drug and alcohol problems and was now in rehab.

"Quite," Siobhan replied. Her dark eyes seeming to look right through Mikey. "Well, I'm sure you have some work to do," she said whilst turning to walk to the front desk, where Tariq was busy sorting out receipts.

Mikey was amazed by himself. He had managed to say what he really thought about the gig last night, instead of doing his usual thing of just agreeing with the other person and keeping what he really thought to himself. He thought Siobhan must have been impressed by his analysis. As, he was sure he saw a nod of approval by her, and she didn't reproach him for what he had said. Inwardly, he delighted in the fact that this was an improvement and a massive step for him. Though, he cautioned calm. As before, he had talked too much and had been told that he thinks he's a know it all and that he must think that he is far superior to everybody else. He knew this was not a good character trait and sought to improve this by holding back at certain points as the person he was talking to, such as Siobhan, would have far more knowledge on the subject they were discussing than he did. He saw a flash on his laptop screen to inform him he had an email in his inbox. He looked up to find

Rachel had gone on a break. So, he busied himself with the new order that had come in.

"Would you mind bringing through the book that Mr Jefferson ordered please, Mikey?" Tariq asked. With his face smiling.

"Sure. Just give me a moment, please," Mikey replied.

"No problem. Bring it through when you're ready," Tariq answered, turning back to the front desk.

"So, your father is originally from Jamaica? And your mother is London born, with an Indian heritage? And you were born in this wonderful town up north? How very interesting," Mr Jefferson was enquiring of Tariq, as Mikey approached with the sticker book. His northeast accent fully in operation.

"Yes, other members of my family originally made the move over in 1948, as part of the Windrush Generation. Though my father came over later and met my mother.

"They moved up here as my dad had a job offer, I was born and the rest as they say, is history," Tariq informed Mr Jefferson, invoking a pleasant smile from both.

"Ahhh Mikey!" Mr Jefferson exclaimed as he approached. "How are you today?"

"I'm well, thank you. How are you?" Mikey managed shyly. Handing over the sticker book to Mr Jefferson. Hoping that he would give him a quick reply and he could slip back to his desk and leave Tariq to deal with the rest of the transaction.

"I'm very well, thank you," Mr Jefferson replied. "We were just talking about our family backgrounds. Have you always lived in Bury, Mikey?"

Instantly Mikey thought about just nodding and leaving it at that. Though, he thought Mr Jefferson might think he was being rude and, he remembered. He told Tariq about his background a

20

while back. He knew he must say something about it, in that case or Tariq may blurt it out instead or, he too might think he is being rude to Mr Jefferson.

"Most of my life, yes. I came here when I was a baby. So, I don't really remember much before that," Mikey replied, hoping that would be enough to satisfy his curiosity.

"Your parents moved you here when you were little, then?" Mr Jefferson politely asked.

"Yes," Mikey answered.

"OK. And all three of us ended up here," Mr Jefferson joked, bellowing out a throaty laugh which rippled his overweight stomach, as he did so. Sensing Mikey's uneasiness with the subject, he turned his attention back to Tariq. "So, Tariq show me what goodies you have for me here, then."

As their attention diverted to the sticker book, Mikey slipped away back to his desk and said to himself; "Don't think about the bad thing. You must not think about the bad thing."

Chapter 2

The rest of the day mundanely passed along without incident. Siobhan had left just before Mr Jefferson had arrived for a meeting with Sean and everybody else got on with business as usual. Rachel and Beth left just before closing, as it was always left up to Mikey and Tariq to close the shop and pull the shutters down. Neither of them minded this and made sure everything was secure before leaving.

"Until tomorrow then, Mikey," Tariq said warmly when the shutters were securely in place.

"See you tomorrow.," Mikey replied and made off for the direction of home. He and Tariq walked opposite ways, so this was their usual goodbyes for the day.

As Mikey walked down the rows of shops on The Rock on his way, he overheard two teenage girls, as he walked past the McDonalds on his left-hand side, discussing 'How fit Harry Styles is'.

"You need to just drink your milkshakes and listen to proper music." Mikey thought to himself as he walked by. As he went further along, he thought he had been a little harsh there and they were entitled to enjoy that kind of thing at their age. He told himself to be a little more understanding of these things.

The warm, early spring sun came upon his face as he approached the turning for his Silver Street apartment. He always had an unnerving sense of dread whenever he got near his apartment on his way home. He always felt that he would walk in to find something had gone terribly wrong, or there would be a letter with bad news awaiting him. He couldn't put his finger on why he felt this. He just had a suspicion that sooner or later, he would find something. He always felt grateful when he walked up the steep steps to his first floor flat and everything was still as he left it. "Another day of freedom," he thought.

As he entered his apartment, he made himself a cup of coffee and went into the living room to sit on the windowsill at the front of the room. This gave him an open view of the opposite side of the street. He liked to sit here and watch the people below mill about and go about their business. He paid particular attention to the bars on the other side. He; himself, had very rarely been into bars or pubs. Only when he had little choice, like going on the works Christmas do, or the times he would attend the gigs of the acts signed to the Energy Label, with his colleagues. Though, he hardly had anything to drink and would just have a couple of weak shandies and they would always be sat away from the main crowd. As he saw a man enter O'Neill's, a bar in full view of his window, he noticed he had just sauntered in, alone. Like he didn't have a care in the world. Mikey was astounded that he was able to do that and wanted to one day be able to do so himself. "It must take such bravery," he thought, to be able to walk into a place full of strangers, with them all looking at you and examining you, without caring in the slightest about what they thought. "I want to do that," he said to himself, aloud this time. "I must be the weakest man alive. I'm twenty-eight years old and I can't even walk into a bar by myself and have a drink. There are no words to describe how much of a shitbag I am. I mean, some days, I don't go to work if I wake up late. As I'm scared of what Sean or Siobhan might say to me. So, I phone and say I'm sick and need the day off. But that just makes it worse, as I must go in the next day and explain myself. I must pretend that I'm still not feeling well and I'm sure, most of the time, they don't believe me. But they don't understand it's after nights I haven't slept and am tired. The last time was when Rachel scolded me for taking too long on a break. There was work to be done, you see. I felt so bad that I went home and couldn't sleep all night. I have to pluck up the courage and go to a bar. I know if I did this, I might be able to feel normal and might realise that I belong amongst society. I have to tell myself that I am good enough and can make a decent life for myself. I wonder what it would be like to join that flock?"

Mikey set his coffee cup down and went to his bedroom to sleep. He needed the comfort of his imaginary dream world.

The first thing he saw when he entered the shop the next morning, was Beth's pretty face and petite frame. She smiled at him and continued to brush her blonde hair and asked, "Have you heard?"

"Heard what?" Mikey replied.

Beth looked up at him, as she had to most people, being below five feet tall. "We have a new starter tomorrow. That's what Siobhan was doing with Sean yesterday. Interviewing him. I'm excited! I love meeting new people," Beth joyfully relayed to Mikey. He had always liked Beth and strangely felt more comfortable with her than anybody else in the shop. She was so sweet and kind. Always a joy to be around and also very sociable. She would be able to adapt to any environment and feel comfortable.

"No, I didn't know," Mikey answered. A nauseating sense of fear coming over him at the thought of having to meet somebody new.

"He's an old school friend of Rachel's," Beth continued.

"Apparently, she said to Siobhan that you guys need more help in the back with the orders we're getting and recommended this guy. Liang is his name. Family is originally from China, I think. It will be good for you to have some male company back there for a change. I know how Rachel can go on at you when you don't do things right. Or take one of your many breaks, as she calls them. I do think she's a little harsh on you sometimes.

"Though, we are here to do a job. I think having him here will be good for you. Don't you think?" Beth asked. Now overwhelmingly displaying her excitement.

"I suppose so," was all Mikey could offer in response, as he felt completely overpowered with the situation.

"Could I have a word with everybody before we open up today, please?" Sean rhetorically asked with authority to the group, as the rest of the team arrived.

Sean Meltzer's six-foot two frame towered over his employees, as they sat waiting for him to speak. A man in his late forties, with receding and greying ginger hair. He cut a figure of authority, though had character traits of somebody who has known how to have a good time in the past.

"As you may or may not have heard," Sean began, "we have a new starter tomorrow. His name is Liang. He is an old school friend of Rachels and comes recommended by her. So, I'm sure he will be a good fit. Siobhan has informed me that we need more help in the back office, dealing with online orders and so forth. The world is changing in that respect. More and more people are buying online, and we need to adapt to that, or we will get left behind. It is important that we focus today and be prepared for when he arrives tomorrow. We need to show him how we work well together, as a team. We can't have anybody late tomorrow, or phoning in sick. We need to be on time, present and have our work heads on. We can't afford for Liang to see us slacking in any way. This means that breaks will be kept to their regular slots and must not run over. This also applies to lunch times. I will be here myself, in the morning tomorrow. After that, I will be leaving you in Siobhan's capable hands for the afternoon. So, let us crack on. Have a good day and make sure we're prepared for tomorrow." Sean smiled his toothy grin, as he watched everybody file to their workplaces.

Mikey spent the rest of the day in a daze.

Chapter 3

His mind had been made up that evening and a decision had been reached. Tonight, would be the night. Mikey climbed into his hot shower and began to firstly shampoo and condition his hair. As he began to lather his Lynx Africa shower gel all over his wet body, an overwhelming sense of nervousness compounded him so much, that he began to physically shake. Though, he felt unbelievably scared, he also felt incredibly excited that he was finally going to do what he had long since wanted.

He decided to keep his choice of clothes casual. He put on a favoured pair of black jeans and blue polo T-shirt. As he descended the steep stairs from his apartment that led to the street, he barely even noticed he was doing so, as the thoughts in his mind were travelling at a speed he struggled to keep up with. He entered Silver Street with his heart pounding in his chest and turned right instead of left. His racing mind told him that he needed a quick walk around the block to prepare himself.

He whirled around turning right at the end of the street, past the HSBC Bank. Followed the path and came to Yates Wine Bar, thirty seconds walk around the corner, directly behind his flat. His stomach churned with fear as he thought about going in. He quickened his pace so he could pass quickly and turn right into Broad Street. Which would bring him full circle and back onto Silver Street. When he reached it, he suddenly turned left instead of right. He needed more time to think. The new plan was to walk this way, past the museum and library to the end. Then cross over the road and turn back. As he got to the end and crossed the road to head back, he thought to himself; "Am I really going to do this?"

He began to walk back as planned and told himself to slow the pace down, as his heart was pounding and his adrenaline flowing. As he approached the bar he could see from his window, he saw people outside smoking. He had hoped this wouldn't be the case and he could have slipped inside without having to pass anybody. His head throbbed with the thought of them saying something to him or mocking him. As he approached, he was met by a massive broad chested man wearing a T-shirt, that made his bicep muscles bulge. Mikey thought immediately of crossing the road, but there was a couple of young ladies stood smoking to the right of him. He realised he was trapped, and the sweat began to appear on his brow.

"Sorry pal, I didn't see you there," the broad chested man said pleasantly to Mikey, as he realised, he was blocking his way.

"No worries, I was just passing," Mikey stammered. Somewhat relieved his worries had come to nothing. The broad chested man just nodded and diverted his attention back to his cigarette and female companions.

Mikey hurried down to the end of the street and turned left onto Bolton Street. He knew if he kept to the left, he would be safe. As the only drinking places were on the right-hand side of the road. He wandered down past the row of takeaways and shops to his left, as if in a dream. Not paying attention to anything or anybody around him. Was this relief? Or was he full of fear from his encounter with the broad chested man. He paid no mind to further thought as he walked past the swimming baths and came to a small grassy area with two benches. Mikey sat upon one of them.

His thoughts turned to what to do next. He knew he couldn't go to a bar now. He would look a fool if he did. All those people who had seen him. Not to mention that man. He seemed friendly enough, Mikey had to concede. Now he had time to reflect on the incident. If the path had been clear and there was nobody outside, he believed he would have walked into O'Neill's bar. It was just unlucky. He thought that next time, he should try to first go somewhere it will be quiet. Mikey reproached himself for being stupid to believe he could just walk into one of the busiest places in town and for it to be okay. Silver Street: after all, is where all the busiest bars are and he only took the apartment there, because it was cheap and all he could afford. Nobody wants to live where the establishments stay open until the early hours if they can help it. Of course, it would not be okay. He was not like other people, was he? That's what he had been told and perhaps they were right. Maybe, there was somewhere on the planet where he fitted in and would feel welcome. Mikey thought it would be best to go back to his apartment and sleep.

He reached the stairs that led to his apartment and ascended them. Hoping as he went, that he would not encounter one of his neighbours from the other flats along the way. This time he didn't. He remembered that the previous day, he was not so lucky. He had encountered Colin. One of the really cocky, sociable types about five years older than Mikey. With his big curly brown hair and massive white pointy teeth, that smile right through your soul when he opened his mouth. His complexion portrayed an obvious regular use of sun beds. He had stopped Mikey in the hall and complained about one of the bulbs in the landing at the top of the stairs having gone and that the estate agents didn't seem interested in replacing it. He then proceeded to try and engage Mikey in general chit chat about how he was doing? How was work? etc. Mikey gave back short, succinct answers. Trying his upmost not to convey his discomfort. They both went their separate ways after that brief encounter and it's difficult to say who was the most relieved.

As Mikey entered his apartment, he said to himself inside his head, "Why can't I be like everybody else?"

Chapter 4

Mikey woke early the next morning. Sean's words about punctuality and attendance still ringing in his ears. He knew he must be perfect today and make a good impression on Liang. He must not let the team down. He threw back the covers on his bed and walked into the bathroom to shower. He prepared himself perfectly that morning and there wasn't a hair out of place, as he left to take the short walk to Energy Records.

When he arrived, he saw that the shutters had already been pulled up and the shop was open. He was hoping that he would be the first one to arrive today. He went inside to find Sean looking through some paperwork. He looked up when he saw Mikey arrive and spoke. "Good morning, Mikey. How are you today?"

"I'm good, thank you. How are you?" Mikey replied.

"I'm excited about today. We have a new starter and I have been thinking that this could be the start of something big for us." Sean beamed. "The online aspect of our business excites me greatly and I feel it is something we need to shift our focus to more and more. It could be our main money earner in the years to come. How do you feel about it?" Sean enquired.

Mikey instantly felt a flush come over him. He told himself to focus. You have prepared yourself perfectly this morning and cannot let the team down. Find the right words.

"I think it's the future of all business," Mikey started. Noticing instantly that Sean wanted a bit more. "I mean, now we have a customer base of older people coming into the shop. Though, all the new; younger customers we get, all buy online. It's rare for one of them to come into the shop and look around. They browse our website instead and purchase what they want from there," he relayed, inwardly delighted that he had managed to give a proper response and that Sean was smiling as he spoke.

"That is exactly what the data told us when Siobhan and I crunched the numbers last week," Sean said proudly. His toothy grin, rearing itself. "You seem to have an insight into this type of thing. That is why I want you to take the lead with Liang today. I want you to show him all aspects of our online work. With your knowledge on this, I see you having a key role in helping this business grow over the next few years," he intently informed his employee.

Mikey was both astounded and delighted by what he had just heard. He had not expected this at all this morning. Or any other morning for that matter. "Thank you, Sean. I hope I can help," was his simple reply. Feeling, for one of the few times in his life, a sense of pride and belonging. He felt a sudden sense of gratitude towards Sean. "He understands me and my value. He has been paying attention to all the hard work I have been putting in and has just been waiting for the right time to tell me. He has found the perfect opportunity now and has taken it. I will not let him down," were the thoughts running through his head after Sean had left the room after saying, "You're welcome and I'm sure you can."

It was work as normal at Energy Records for the first hour of business, as Liang was not due to arrive until 10am. When Rachel had arrived, she had gone immediately to speak to Siobhan and had not given Mikey a second glance. He hoped that everything was okay with her, as she didn't seem pleased at all.

When Liang arrived just before ten, he was greeted by Siobhan and taken upstairs to where her and Sean's offices were. Those offices were places that the rest of them very rarely went up to, unless summoned. Or, had something important to tell either Siobhan or Sean. Which was not often the case for Mikey. Rachel went up to see Siobhan more often than any of them and Mikey assumed they had important things to discuss. A smile came across his face when he realised that he too would now have important business to discuss with her as well, going forward. After what he had been told this morning. He knew he needed to keep his head down this morning and get through as much work as possible. Then, he would be fully prepared to show Liang the ropes this afternoon. For as with any new starter, which Mikey was himself some eighteen months ago, would spend the morning upstairs with Sean and Siobhan going through all aspects of the job and what was expected of them. The afternoon would then be spent on the shop floor or in the back, depending on their job role.

Mikey was enjoying his beef and horseradish sandwich from Tesco for his lunch, one of his favourites, when Siobhan arrived at his desk and engaged him. "Hi Mikey, I just wanted to have a quick word about this afternoon with you."

"Ok, no problem," Mikey replied, setting aside his sandwich.

"I just want to make sure that you know what you need to do this afternoon," she began, folding her hands into an embrace with each other. "Sean has informed me that he wants you to take the lead with Liang and show him the ropes. Now, it is important that he is shown the proper way we do things here and not your way of using shortcuts. As we both know, that leads to the mistakes you make. I want your full concentration on this, Mikey.

So, that means the correct working structure must be adhered to. If there are no new orders coming in later in the afternoon and you are struggling for work to show him. I want you to think outside the box and think of something for him to do. I don't want him thinking it's okay to wander off on breaks willy nilly just because there are no orders coming in. Am I clear about this?" Siobhan asked in a low, though stern voice.

"Yes. I will show him everything correctly and only take a break for fifteen minutes, at three. I will go through everything," Mikey slowly responded. His voice beginning to waver at the end.

"Good. Let him leave at four-thirty and come up to my office to discuss how you got on before you leave for the day, please," she ordered him.

"Yes, no problem," he murmured.

"Good luck," Siobhan said as she left the room.

"Thank you," Mikey responded to her back.

Mikey sat at his desk making sure everything was perfect and looked in his inbox and was delighted to see several orders waiting. "Fantastic," he thought, "I will have stuff to do with him and show him."

"Don't just sit there, Mikey," Rachel teased as she gave him a playful punch on the shoulder.

"I'm just looking at what I can show him," Mikey responded, looking up from his computer screen, noticing Rachel had a full face of makeup and a low-cut top on.

She leaned forward and asked, "How do I look?"

"You look nice, Rachel." Mikey blushed.

"Thank you, kind sir," Rachel exulted. "It is always very important to make a good first impression in life. Even though, I used to go to school with Liang, we haven't spent any real time together since. I chanced seeing him in a bar down Deansgate about a month back. That was the first time we've seen each other since. He said he was unemployed, so I recommended him for here. Siobhan was a bit of a bitch about it.

Saying we don't need the extra staff. She's a bit of a dick. Don't you think? Always on at us for taking breaks and making mistakes. I mean, me mostly. She never praises me for anything and just criticises me. Oh well, just because she's old and sad," she went on. Preening herself.

The conversation was abruptly interrupted, as Sean entered alongside Siobhan and Liang.

"Liang this is Rachel, who I know you already have acquaintance with from your high school days. And this is Mikey. He has been with us for just over eighteen months now and he will be showing you your primary duties today and taking charge of your training. Siobhan and I will leave it in your capable hands, Mikey. I will see you in the morning." Sean structurally informed him before nodding to everybody in turn and leaving the room. With Siobhan following in tow.

"Stop the trembles! Stop the trembles! You must be perfect! You must be perfect!" Mikey shouted at his body through his mind.

"Hi Liang. Please have a seat next to me here," Mikey invited. More calmly than he had expected.

Mikey proceeded to take the new starter through the roles and responsibilities of the job for the next hour. Save for the interruptions of Rachel, to talk about their old school days and the times her, Liang and others used to go underage drinking on a park near where they lived. "Those were the days," she declared.

"Do you want to come for a cigarette break with me?" Rachel then timidly asked Liang, at just after 2pm.

"Isn't it a bit early yet?" Mikey queried of Rachel.

"It's okay. It's his first day and you've filled his head with a lot of information," Rachel responded.

Liang looked at Mikey who just nodded and he rose to leave with Rachel. Mikey prayed upon all hope the whole time they were gone, that Siobhan would not come down from her office and notice what was happening.

This went on for the rest of the afternoon, with two more extra cigarette breaks before Mikey let Liang go for the day, as planned, and went up to report to Siobhan.

He reported to her that Liang seemed bright, intelligent and that he seemed to take everything on board. He concluded that he would be capable of doing the job and would fit in well with the rest of the team. He did tell her that there was one extra cigarette break, at Rachel's insistence. Due to Liang having to take a lot of information on board. Siobhan thought that was acceptable, as Rachel is a good judge of these things and informed him that it seemed he had done a good job.

He said his traditional goodbye to Tariq upon the closing of the shop. For once, on his way home, Mikey had a sense of joy and adrenaline in his stomach.

Chapter 5

"Yesterday was absolutely unbelievable, Siobhan," Rachel fumed as they sat in the Costa Coffee, situated less than a hundred yards from Energy Records. "That's why I text you last night and asked to meet this morning. So, we could speak before anything else goes wrong today. I mean, what must Liang have thought of us?" Rachel continued stirring her latte.

"I want you to tell me what happened," Siobhan said calmly, sitting completely still and allowing Rachel the time to think about what she wanted to say.

She composed herself and began. "When Liang arrived and Mikey started training him, everything was fine. He was showing him through the website and our database. Then went on to how our server allows us to all interact with each other. What marketing tools we use to pinpoint potential customers. Then, he started bumbling all over himself and I had to interject and tell stories about our school days together. So, Mikey could recompose himself. It was cringy. Mikey then suggested that I take Liang out for a cigarette break. I told him it was a bit early, but he insisted. Then, when he was showing him how we deal with the orders that come in online; well, that was a massive load of his lazy techniques and shortcuts. I really, really wanted to say something, but I knew that would undermine him and I didn't want to do that. He told me to take Liang out for two further cigarette breaks, while he tried to figure out what to do with him. As he was clearly running out of ideas. I told you yesterday morning that I wasn't sure if he would be up to doing the training…"

Sensing Rachel could go on at length on the subject and satisfied she had all the knowledge she needed. Siobhan interjected. "I think I have a clear enough picture and that was not the feedback Mikey gave to me yesterday. I will give it some thought and see how he gets on the rest of the week. Then, decide if I need to speak to Sean," she concluded. Getting up from the table. "Ok. Thank you for your input, as always Rachel. I do appreciate your hard work for this company."

"Thank you, Siobhan." Rachel beamed. "You and Sean are the best people to work for," she complimented. Showing her winner of a smile.

Mikey was stood with Liang and Tariq when Siobhan and Rachel entered the shop before opening time. Playing a minor role in the conversation, as they began the process of getting to know each other. Liang was telling the story how he had worked the last summer as a holiday rep in Ibiza. Boasting how the girls were all over him when they knew he could get them tickets for all the best night clubs. "I got all the best pussy on the island, mate." Liang revelled in telling his audience.

"I don't doubt it, Mate. Chicks dig a guy who can get her into top clubs and shit," Tariq responded, clearly excited by the subject. "I would love to do it one summer, mate. Just let me go and partay brother!" He laughed. Raising his voice half an octave.

"What about you, Mikey?" Liang asked, turning to face him.

"Not really sure it's Mikey's scene," Tariq joked, giving Mikey a playful dig in the ribs.

Mikey had so far kept on the periphery of the conversation when it had turned from work and what was needed to be done that day on to a more jovial personal conversation, which he struggled to keep up with and felt uncomfortable with. He would normally try to slip away unnoticed in these situations. Though, with his sense of achievement yesterday and aligned, with his willingness to make good on his promise to Sean, he endeavoured to stay and make a fist of staying in the conversation as best he could. He felt incredibly anxious now. Especially after Tariq's jibe and willed his mind to think of something to say.

"Could I have a word before you start, please Mikey?" Siobhan asked pleasantly. Knowing she didn't need an invitation to interrupt the conversation.

"My fucking hero!" Mikey exclaimed silently inside his head.

"Yes, sure," was all he said. Following Siobhan into the back room towards his desk.

"Sit down please," Siobhan instructed.

Mikey did as he was bid. Feeling a real uneasiness coming over him and he started to panic. Thinking this can only be bad news. Nothing good can come of this. I can tell by the look on her face, that she is not happy. "Keep yourself together!" he ordered himself, inside his head.

"I will keep this short as we haven't much time," Siobhan began. "I understand yesterday would have been a new experience for you, as you have never had the responsibility of training somebody before. I just wanted to say that I need focus from you today. Have a good day," she finished with and left the room, smiling to Rachel and Liang as they entered.

Mikey was very confused. He didn't know what to think. For some reason, he had expected a tongue lashing from Siobhan at that moment. Though none was forthcoming. He knew that he did a good job yesterday and deserved praise instead of criticism. He had received neither. He was just told to focus. Was this indirect praise? Like, you did a good job yesterday and just make sure you stay focused today? Or, or was it that cigarette break he told her about? Is that why she had told him to stay focused? So, there would be no more of them? I expect she has told the same thing to Rachel, in that case. As it was her idea. She must have. That's why he saw them both arrive together this morning. She would have told her before they got here, to save her embarrassment. Like, she had just done with him. What did she say? "I will keep this short as we haven't much time?" Yes! That's it! She has told us both that we did a good job yesterday, but to stay focused and cut out the extra breaks. In a nice polite way, that keeps our spirits up. That's great management. He endeavoured that he must protect Rachel and keep focused today.

The morning passed by in the blink of an eye for Mikey that day. It was the busiest morning he had experienced in several months, due to a targeted online ad campaign that Sean had put together. Requests and orders were streaming in and there wasn't any time for any extra breaks. With both he and Rachel working flat out to keep up.

The orders kept coming in thick and fast. The campaign that went out last night, was really working. To such an extent, that Beth offered to help with the extra workload. Mikey accepted that this was a good idea, and they could do with the help. On the rare occasions he got chance to work with Beth, he really enjoyed it. She was always so calm and hard working. She radiated intelligence, which Mikey admired. She is the type of person who picks things up very quickly. Only must be told how to do something once before she grasps it. Now in her mid-twenties, she has a steady boyfriend who she shares an apartment with, about fifteen minutes' walk from town. Given the fact that she is studying for her psychology degree in the evenings, it is no surprise how bright she is.

As the afternoon went on, Liang asked. "Why don't you let me loose on a few? I feel as if I'm ready."

"That's a good idea, Mikey," Rachel agreed. "Just give him the simple ones for now and we can deal with the others," she offered. "No offence, Liang. Only as it's your first time," she spoke, winking and patting Liang's arm.

Although, hard work was done by all that afternoon. Beth and Mikey did the majority. Mikey put that down to the fact that Liang was new, and it was Rachel who; that afternoon, was mainly working with him and laughing and joking with, as they went. Mikey thought he must be a really funny guy, with lots of interesting things to say. As they spent some of the afternoon, laughing, joking, and just talking. They spent their breaks together smoking and took more time than they should. Mikey thought that this was acceptable, and Siobhan wouldn't mind, considering the work load they had on.

"Wow! You guys had a busy day, today," Tariq commented to Mikey as they were closing.

"Yeah, that campaign of Sean's really seems to have worked," Mikey replied. Still in a bit of a daze from the day's work.

"Bet you could do with a beer, hey?" Tariq asked amusedly. "I'm definitely having some with the missus tonight. And not just the beer!" He laughed, throwing out a hearty grin.

"Yeah," Mikey replied.

"Until tomorrow, then," said Tariq.

"Until tomorrow," Mikey replied.

It was strangely quiet as a churchyard as Mikey walked down The Rock, back home. "Everybody must be on their computers, buying from our website," he joked to himself as he walked.

As he came upon the crossing with the HSBC bank opposite, which led to his own street. He walked a little further along and stood outside Wyldes. A bar more or less adjacent to the bank, on the opposite side of the road. He asked himself, "Should I?"

"Not tonight. But soon," he concluded in his head and made his way to his apartment.

There he encountered Colin, clearly drunk, trying to get his key into the communal door at the bottom of the stairs to the apartments.

"Mikey!" Colin bellowed when he saw him. "Can you help us, mate?" he slurred, struggling to stand.

"Sure," replied Mikey, opening the door with his key with one hand and holding Colin up with the other.

As he helped him up the stairs, Colin told Mikey all about how he had a fantastic day drinking and betting in the bookies. How he had won fifty quid and spent it all in the boozer. "Getting well and truly, wankered," was the description he gave.

As they reached Colin's apartment, Mikey took his keys from him and opened the door, before handing them back and making sure he got inside.

"You're a good lad you, Mikey. Sound. Sound as a pound, you Mikey. A little dull and quiet maybe. But salt of the earth, you are. You should come drinking with me one day. I will show you what fun is, matey!" Colin slobbered over Mikey as he entered his apartment.

"Good night, mate," he ended with before closing the door.

"Good night," Mikey reciprocated to the closed door.

"Well. I thought I was strange," Mikey murmured out loud as he entered his own apartment.

Chapter 6

The next couple of days went similarly by as the rest of the week. With things progressively tailing off as the week progressed. Beth had gone back to her role on the front desk with Tariq. Once satisfied the three remaining in the back were sufficient to deal with the workload. Mikey spent more and more time dealing with orders on his own, as the week went on. He didn't mind this as it seemed to him that Rachel and Liang worked well together and if this was the best way to get the work done, then so be it.

"We need to wait for the next wave," was the conclusion Sean came to on Friday morning when addressing the decline in online orders and enquiries over the course of the week. He also urged them, "To keep a tally of everybody you communicate with and whether they bought, or not. If they didn't, I want to understand a flavour of the reasons why."

One incident that had occurred on Saturday, made Mikey smile as he reminisced about it over his Sunday morning coffee. He had been told by Sean that Reggie, the new electrician was coming in to fix a few things that needed attention. He had told Mikey to let Siobhan know that he was coming, as this would be the first time Reggie had done jobs at the shop and they had never met before. However, Reggie had arrived as Mikey and Tariq were opening the shop and he had no time to tell Siobhan before she arrived. A small; dreadlocked man, who instantly displayed his dry humour upon meeting him. He told Mikey. "I will be out of your hair in no time," and joked, "where's the boss man? I bet he can't be arsed to come in on no Saturday, can he?" Laughing and showing a gap-toothed smile.

Mikey didn't really know how to respond to that. So, he just smiled and laughed a long with him and quietly replied. "Yeah, just us today."

It was then that Siobhan arrived and instantly asked Reggie condescendingly, "And who are you?"

"I'm the finest electrician in the land," Reggie smirked and mocked back. "And who might you be?"

"I'm the manager of this store," Siobhan hotly asserted.

"Well, that's that settled then." Reggie grinned. "You can go and manage and I will fix your little electrical problems and be out of your hair."

Siobhan briefly looked at Mikey, before slipping off upstairs to her office.

"She always so far up her own arse?" Reggie asked. When Siobhan had disappeared behind her office door.

"Always, mate," Tariq answered before Mikey could even think to utter a response.

Remembering this, Mikey realised it had amused him so much because he had never heard anybody speak to Siobhan in that manner before. He knew now that she deserved it and could have handled the situation a lot better. She could have been more tactful in enquiring to Reggie who he was. Better still, she should have said nothing to him and then asked either himself, or Tariq what he was doing there. For the first time, he realised that Siobhan had been pretty rude to Reggie, and he didn't deserve it. Did she see him dressed the way he was, in dirty overalls and somehow think she was better than him? Did his rough south Manchester accent, make her more refined one, feel more superior? Even if any of this was the case, you should never look down on somebody. Especially when he had come to do an important job in making sure the shop could function correctly. Mikey asked himself. "If our electricity went down and Reggie wasn't there to fix it. Would the shop be able to open?" Of course, no was the answer to that. So, everybody has just as an important role to play in a business. Regardless of whether you're the manager, the director, or the tea boy. Nobody should look down on anybody unless they're admiring their shoes. He thought. "A razor blade is sharp, though can't cut down a tree. An axe is strong, though can't cut your hair." Everybody has their own role to play, which is unique and of equal importance.

Mikey spent the rest of his Sunday afternoon, watching Game of Thrones. He had collected all the DVDs of the first three series and was eagerly awaiting the release of the fourth. Just before he fell into a snooze on his couch, which was a regular occurrence for him. He heard Tyrion Lannister remark. "Where is the God of tits and wine? We shall pray to him and serve him well."

"Indeed," Mikey thought before drifting off to sleep.

Chapter 7

"Wow! We've had a lot of orders and queries in over the weekend, Liang," Mikey relayed when he opened his inbox first thing on that Monday morning.

Liang turned to face him and said point blank, "Mikey, I know just as much as you about this job now and don't need to listen to you anymore. I know exactly what I am doing. You're not my manager. So, let me get on with my job."

Mikey was stunned. His lips trembled for a response. He looked at Liang for a time, trying to think of something to say. His words absolutely failed him. He felt he should be angry at this rebuff, though the way Liang had spoken to him, scared him. He slowly turned; ashen faced, back towards his laptop screen. Feeling crestfallen and had a lack of understanding as to why he had been spoken to in this manner. Had he done something to upset Liang? He couldn't think of anything. Sure, he had allowed him to work more closely with Rachel over the past few days. That was only because they had been busy, and they seemed to work well together.

As Rachel arrived for the day, she said a quick "Good morning," to Tariq and Beth in turn and headed straight upstairs to Siobhan's office.

"Good morning, Rachel. How was your weekend?" Siobhan greeted her with. Once she had knocked and entered, offering her a seat across the desk.

"It was good, thank you. Me and some girlfriends went down

to Deansgate Locks in Manchester on Saturday night and Sunday was spent recovering." Rachel recalled, taking the seat offered.

"Good. As long as you had fun. A young lady like you should be having fun." Siobhan smiled back. "Oh, I could tell you some stories of my younger days, hanging out and getting up to mischief." She dreamed, thinking of days gone by.

"I bet you could!" Rachel exclaimed. "I bet you could still teach us young ones a thing or two!" She warmly effused smiling and receiving one back in return.

"I could literally sit and talk to you all day about it. However, we need to talk about how Liang is coming along and how Mikey is dealing with his training?" Siobhan imparted. Bringing the conversation back to the matter at hand.

"Liang is fabulous!" Rachel preened. "If I can borrow one of your wonderful phrases?" she shyly enquired.

"Of course. Fabulous is a word that states your emotion on a subject perfectly," Siobhan responded. Clearly enjoying the compliment. "Now, what about Mikey? And his handling of the situation?"

"Non-existent," Rachel relayed hotly. "He hardly even speaks to him anymore. He has just left it all on me to deal with. I mean; if I had been told to look after his training, I wouldn't mind at all. But, seen as Sean told Mikey to do it and Liang has picked it up really fast. He will get all the credit for it, and I see that as unfair," she told Siobhan with an upset expression over her pretty face.

"Do you think he is incapable? Or just plainly can't be bothered?" Siobhan asked.

"I think it's a bit of both," Rachel responded.

"Okay," Siobhan interjected. As Rachel was about to go on. "I will speak to Sean about it and let him know that it was you, who has done most of the training with Liang. I will see what he says about Mikey," she conveyed. In a matter-of-fact way.

"Thank you," Rachel meekly responded.

"No, thank you Rachel," Siobhan replied. "You are my special girl and a big asset to this company. Now, keep this to yourself and have a good day." She warmly smiled to Rachel.

"Thank you and the same to you." Rachel smiled back before getting up to leave the office and make the walk downstairs to her workstation.

"Good morning, Mikey," she greeted him as he stood pouring himself a cup of coffee from the machine in the kitchen, to the side of the back office. "How was your weekend?"

"It was good, thank you," Mikey responded.

"What did you get up to?" she enquired. Getting a bottle of water from the fridge.

"Just watched Game of Thrones and chilled," he hesitantly confided.

"Boring," she teased.

"I went down Deansgate and lived it up. Is Liang in yet?" she asked.

"Yes," Mikey replied. The question bringing back the memory of the conversation from earlier.

"Good," she responded already on her way to the back office. Seemingly no longer aware of Mikey's presence.

"I told him," Liang whispered, as she entered.

"Good. I told Siobhan. What did he say?" she asked enthusiastically.

"Nothing. Just stared for a little bit and turned back to his screen," Liang mocked. "He always stares at that screen. Like it has magic powers, or something."

"I told you he was a wuss, didn't I?" Rachel laughed.

48

Revelling in the fact that her plan had come to fruition. "Shush! He's coming." She cut Liang off, as he was about to reply.

Mikey felt uneasy sitting at his desk and starting work that morning. He knew some of it had to do with what Liang had said to him. But there was something else. An atmosphere he couldn't put his finger on. The tectonic plates of his world had shifted somehow, and he didn't know as to which destination they were heading.

"How are you feeling today, Mikey?" Beth asked. Appearing in the back office when Mikey was there alone. With Rachel and Liang having gone for one of their morning cigarette breaks.

"I'm okay, Beth. Thank you," Mikey responded. Not knowing what else to say.

"You just seem a little on edge today, is all," Beth softly and kindly spoke. With a real warmth and concern.

"I'm doing all right, thanks. I'm just a little tired. Didn't get much sleep last night." Mikey slowly replied. Feeling the warmth and kindness shown and appreciating it. He struggled, as he desperately didn't want to hurt her feelings. He wanted to tell her how he was really feeling. But he couldn't find the words. Maybe, he didn't really know himself.

"Okay," Beth kindly stated. "If you ever need to talk about anything; or have something on your mind, you can tell me, Mikey. You're a great guy, who is fantastic at his job, and I don't like to see you upset," she tried to coax.

"Thank you, Beth. I appreciate it." Mikey found himself smiling back at her. His shoulder blades shifted their load with what he had just heard. She really was a kind and gentle soul, who wanted the best for him. He thought. "Maybe she understands me. Have I just let her down and hurt her? By not expressing how I feel?"

"Just one more thing," Beth announced before she left the room, "You need to say something about Rachel and Liang going for cigarette breaks together. It's not fair for them to leave you alone for long periods, to do all the work."

"Okay," is all Mikey managed.

"It's a disgusting habit anyway. You're better well away from it." Beth laughed as she left.

"What did Beth want?" Rachel asked. As she and Liang walked back into the office. Having seen her leave as they entered the shop.

"Just seeing what I was doing for lunch," Mikey lied. Feeling the need to protect Beth.

"Subway today, I reckon," Liang interjected, with the enthusiasm of a child.

"Good shout!" Rachel high fived him.

"Just Tesco for me, I think," Mikey dully replied.

"Boring, as usual," Rachel mocked.

As the working day ended and everybody else had gone on home; Mikey suddenly blurted out to Tariq as they locked up. "I'm having a fucking beer, tonight."

"Good lad!" Tariq enthused. "It's about time you let your hair down."

"Yeah, you're not wrong there." Mikey replied. Almost oblivious to Tariq's presence.

"Until tomorrow then, my fellow little wreck 'ead!" Tariq joked.

"Wouldn't go that far, Tariq. Just a couple," Mikey cautioned.

"I know mate, just joking with you. Have fun and see you tomorrow." Tariq fist bumped him as he spoke.

"Until tomorrow, Tariq."

"You are okay. You will be fine. Do not think of the bad thing. Do not think of the bad thing. Nothing good ever comes of that." Mikey told himself in his head, as he walked down The Rock after leaving work for the day.

In those moments, he could not tell you anything about his surroundings of where he was heading and how he would get there. He was completely lost in the thoughts of his mind. Walking completely on auto pilot.

"Imagine the joy I would feel if I never thought about the bad thing again," he mused. "Imagine that it was a thing of the past. A relic, a fossil. Not to be admired and studied like great things from the past. To stand as a warning for how not to treat people. That would be the greatest thing to ever happen," he concluded as he walked past the church which stood on his right-hand side.

He continued to walk the fifty yards or so, to reach the crossing for his street. He did not cross. He walked straight past Wyldes and stood outside The Old White Lion pub next door. He stood for a moment and surveyed the scene. All was quiet. Trembling, he pushed the door to the establishment open. To his dismay, he found that this was no ordinary door. It was a revolving type, that you would find outside hotels or shopping centres. "Do not fall over," he ordered himself as he struggled with the concept of how to get to the other side of the moving entry way. Finally, he made it through and began the short walk towards the bar area. A quick look around told him that it was quiet. Only about four people there. "That's good," he thought. As his feet felt the change from carpet to the tiles that surrounded the bar area.

"Yes, love?" was the question posed by the barmaid. A

woman he estimated to be in her mid-thirties.

"You didn't think of that, did you? You absolute fool!" He chastised himself in his head.

"Same again. When you're ready please, Sue," was the voice of a tall man, with grey hair and beard approaching the bar. This gave Mikey time to think.

"Erm… a pint of Carlsberg, please?" he hesitantly managed. Thinking one pint would be okay. For some reason, he felt asking for a shandy would have been embarrassing.

Sue silently began to pour the drink and brought it back to set it in front of Mikey when she had finished and spoke, "Two pound eighty, please."

Mikey wordlessly paid her a five-pound note and waited for his change. When he received it back in his hand, he uttered. "Thank you," and turned to look for a seat.

He saw the seats to his right, near the front window were free. There was nobody in that part of the pub. "Perfect," he thought and made his way over there.

He sat in the corner, which gave him a full view out of the front window and took a hesitant first sip of his beer. His right-hand trembling on the glass. He had to use his left to steady it. He took another sip shortly after. A little calmer this time. He gazed outside the window and saw people going about their daily business. Turned his head slightly and realised he could see the communal entrance to his apartment from here. "Not far to go," he thought as he took a third sip. After which, he cautioned himself to slow down.

His thoughts then turned to the events of his day at work. He thought about what Liang had said to him and realised that it had really annoyed him. "How dare he speak to me in that manner!" he furiously said in his head. "Am I that worthless? That somebody who has only been doing the job for a week knows it better than me? I know he has picked it up quickly and has done well. But so did I when I first started. I remember Sean saying that nobody had picked it up as quickly as me when I ended my first week. Should I say something to him? No, I can't. That would upset Rachel.

He is her friend, and she doesn't deserve that. She does go on sometimes, but she is kind to me at other times as well. Maybe I just need to be better at my work? No, that's not it. I am good at my job and could do it standing on my head. I need to be better at the social side of things. That's it! Tell some jokes and funny stories about things I've done. I don't have any stories though. I'm sad. I just go about my life in a zombie state, most of the time. Why can't I just be normal and be like everybody else? Because I'm dirty! I always got myself dirty! Dirty! A dirty boy! I must get in that tub and scrub myself! I am a dirty boy, and nobody loves me! That's why your parents abandoned you and I'm stuck with you! Stuck with a dirty boy! Oh no! The bad thing! The bad thing! Why did I come here? Why did I think it would be okay? Get up and leave!" Mikey began to shake as he put his hand on his glass, to take it back to the bar.

"Mikey!!!" Was the bellow from a man, approaching his table. Bringing his thoughts instantly back into the room. In somewhat of a daze.

"What are you doing in here?" Mr Jefferson asked. Sitting down at the table. "Just, just having a quick drink," Mikey stammered.

"I've never seen you in here before. Where do you normally drink?" Mr Jefferson politely asked.

"I don't really," Mikey muttered.

"What brings you in here, today?" Mr Jefferson enquired

quizzically.

"Just fancied a drink," was all Mikey could think of as a response.

"Now, that was a good idea. Stay and have another one with me. I'm buying! What are you on there? Carlsberg? I will get a round in." Mr Jefferson announced. Standing up to go to the bar.

"Well, I can't leave now, can I? It would be rude if I did. What if he told Sean or Siobhan? He is one of our best customers." Mikey pondered whilst Mr Jefferson was at the bar.

"How's the new starter getting on at your place?" Mr Jefferson asked. Retaking his seat at the table, directly across from Mikey.

"Well," Mikey responded. Giving off a slight flash of irritation at the mention of Liang. He hoped it hadn't been noticed. It had.

"You're not keen on him, are you?" Mr Jefferson questioned. Already knowing the answer.

"He's okay, I suppose." Mikey lied. Hoping that would be enough to satisfy. It would not.

"Mikey, please take a bit of advice from an old fool." Mr Jefferson began. "You won't get on with everybody you work with. People in your life in general, for whatever reason as well. Sometimes, you just must grin and bear it. You are a wonderful young man. I know that from the dealings I've had with you. There is no reason not to like you. So, this Liang fella might be a bit of a wrong 'un. But sometimes you must pretend. Don't blow smoke up his arse and be two faced. Just be civil and get through as painlessly as possible. It's best for everybody concerned. You get my drift?"

Mikey saw a seriousness to Mr Jefferson's face, that he had never seen before and realised he was teaching him an important life lesson in this moment. He decided to just nod his head and try to take it in.

"I will be keeping an eye on this fella when I'm in your shop. If I see him being the clown. I will let him know about it," Mr Jefferson seriously promised him. "You need to learn to protect yourself and your own feelings when you're in the workplace and everywhere else as well, for that matter. Your mind is the most important tool that you possess. You need to protect it at all costs, from those who want to harm it," he continued. The wisdom flowing now.

"I will try, I promise." Mikey replied. With a huge sense of gratitude towards his companion. He felt connected to Mr Jefferson in that moment. He realised that he must have sensed he was upset and was giving him this advice, not only to make him feel better. To also teach him lessons in how to cope with situations and life in general, for that matter, better. He felt a real warmth towards him then and before thinking about it asked. "Another one, Mr Jefferson?"

"Why not?" Mr Jefferson answered, heartily laughing. "You can call me Tom and not be so formal," he added.

The drinks began to flow freely after that and gradually, so did the conversation. Mr Jefferson told Mikey stories of how he used to be 'A bit of a rascal'when he worked at the car plant up in the Northeast before moving down here after he retired. He taught Mikey to be wary of employers trying to exploit him. "The fuckers will take every ounce of flesh you have if you let them. Take your gaffer, Seany boy. Smiles a lot, doesn't he? He's got some arrogance about him, that one. But, where he lacks is, that he doesn't listen. He hears, but he doesn't listen. There is a massive difference.

He thinks he listens, but he is only hearing. He makes his

mind up on something and that is his agenda and won't sway from it. That is his downfall. You must make him listen. He will if you say the right words," Mr Jefferson went on. Mikey listened incredulously. He was stunned by his analysis.

Mr Jefferson enquired a lot as to his upbringing and as the beer had well and truly taken over by that point, Mikey opened up about the fact that he was adopted when he was six months old and doesn't know anything about his parents. Save for the fact that they abandoned him and left him to be brought up by other people, though his adopted mother had died of cancer when he was four and his adopted father was the one to bring him up for the rest of his childhood. He told him how upon his sixteenth birthday, his adopted father told him to leave his home and fend for himself. He then lived in shelters for the next few years, before nailing down a job in a factory and managing to get his own place. Then ended up starting at Energy Records.

"Don't ever believe that you have not achieved anything with your life," was how Mr Jefferson had responded to the story. "After what you have told me, you are one of the strongest people I have ever met. To come through that and grow into the amazing young man sat before me today. You should feel immensely proud of yourself," Mr Jefferson crowed. Putting his hand on his shoulder.

The night finished as Sue called for last orders and they finished their drinks. Mikey walked Mr Jefferson to the taxi rank a few metres down the road to get a cab home and turned to him and said, as his taxi arrived. "Thank you, Mr erm, Tom. Thank you for tonight. I really appreciate it."

"Anytime, Mikey. Anytime," Mr Jefferson warmly responded, before getting into his taxi.

Mikey made the short walk back to his apartment, drunk.

Though, extremely satisfied with how the night had turned out after all.

He walked into his apartment and started singing to himself, "Cheese 'n' chive, Won't you…? Be my Valentine? I said cheeeese 'n' chiiive Be myyyy Valentiiine!"

Chapter 8

"I gave him that opportunity, to prove himself," Sean was saying to Siobhan in their meeting in his office he had called her into that morning. "The feedback from you is that he has basically left it all up to Rachel to deal with the new starter. That was after the first day?" he asked.

"Correct," Siobhan simply responded.

"What is on my radar now, is that he has called in sick today and I need to understand the reason for that. Is it because he is genuinely ill? Or if there is something else going on," Sean informed her. Thinking about his options.

Sensing this, Siobhan asked. "How would you like me to help you with this?"

"I'm going to have a chat with everybody separately today and see where the land lies after that," Sean decided. "I want you to sit in on these meetings and I will be asking you for your feedback, after they have concluded. Please ask Rachel to come up first," he politely ordered, nodding his head towards the door.

"Have a seat please, Rachel." Sean beckoned as Rachel entered his office with Siobhan. She silently took a seat across the desk from Sean. With Siobhan sitting to her left and Sean's right at the corner of his desk.

"Good morning. How are you today?" Sean began.

"I'm very well, thank you. I'm excited by the new work we have on and loving how it keeps me busy all day. How are you, Sean?" Rachel creamed. Suggestively asking the question at the end.

"It makes me pleased that you are dedicated to your job," Sean professionally replied. "I have called you in here today. Because as you know, Mikey has called in sick. I want to ask first, how he has been with Liang since he started?"

"Well, I have already raised concerns with Siobhan about this," Rachel started. Looking across to her manager.

"I know. Now I want you to tell me. In your own words and how you see it," Sean interrupted.

"Well, I mean. I don't want to get him into trouble." Rachel began shyly. Looking down at her embraced fingers.

"It's not a question of that. I just need your honest feedback," Sean informed her.

"Ok. Well, he has taken less and less notice of him as the days have gone by," she started. "The first hour or so on Liang's first day was fine. Then, he started to bumble all over himself. So, he asked me to help by taking Liang out for extra cigarette breaks, while he tried to think of something to do with him. As the week went on, he took less, and less interest and it was left to me to deal with Liang's training. As I said to Siobhan, I don't mind that. I am more than happy to go the extra mile for this company as, you're amazing to work for. I think it was a combination of not being up to the job of doing the training. Maybe, because he's never done it before. And seeming like he couldn't be bothered, especially when Beth came in to help us with the extra work. He lost all interest then and spent all his time working with her and laughing and joking with her. Sending us two out for more breaks. I'm guessing, so he could spend time alone with her."

"Ok, thank you. I think I have enough of a picture on that," Sean interrupted. "Now, I want to move on to yesterday. Did

Mikey tell you anything about what he was doing after work?" he asked.

"He didn't say anything to me, though Tariq told me that he told him that he was going to go out, get drunk and sink at least ten pints. I think he told him this when they were locking up for the day," Rachel recalled, trying to look deep into her memory.

"Ok. Thank you for your time. I will let you know if I need anything further," Sean concluded.

"You're welcome, Sean. I'm glad to help," Rachel innocently replied. Giving a look and a smile to Siobhan when she stood up to leave. Which was reciprocated.

"What do you think?" Siobhan asked after Rachel had left.

"I want to speak to Tariq. Tell him to come up, please," Sean ordered Siobhan.

"Tariq, please sit down. How are you today?" Sean asked. As Tariq seated himself in the same place as Rachel had. With, Siobhan taking her seat back.

"I'm doing good, thank you. How about you?" Tariq jovially asked.

"I'm okay. I just have something to ask you regarding Mikey." Sean began.

"OK." Tariq nodded.

"As you know he has phoned in sick today, and I want to know if you spoke about anything as you locked the shop up last night?" Sean asked. Looking intently at him. Searching his reaction to the question.

"Yeah, we spoke about what we were doing that night," Tariq responded. Knowing what question might be next and stalling for a bit of time to think.

"What did he say he was doing?" Sean asked. Point blank.

"I wasn't really paying that much attention as my missus was calling my mobile at the same time." Tariq lied. "He did say something about having a couple of beers," he had to concede. Feeling the pressure of the situation.

"So, he said he was going for a couple of beers that night?" Sean enquired with surprise.

"I'm not sure if he meant that night, or the weekend. Like I say, I was distracted at the time and I'm sorry, Sean. I didn't think at the time that it was that important," Tariq replied. More feverishly as he went on.

"Ok, Tariq. Thank you." Sean calmed him. "Have you noticed anything about his work that has given you cause for concern?" he asked.

"I don't really work in the back that much, but I know things have been said in the past, that he can be work shy sometimes and make mistakes. Though, like I say, I don't really work with him that often to comment properly." Tariq uneasily answered.

"Ok. I think I have everything I need from you, for now," Sean decided. "If you remember anything more about your conversation last night, I want you to tell me," he ordered looking directly at Tariq.

"I will do," Tariq promised.

"Thank you." Sean nodded to him as he quickly rose and left the room.

"Let's see what Beth has to say. Can you bring her up, please?" Sean asked of Siobhan.

Beth sat in the same seat as her two colleagues and Sean began. "Hi Beth, how are you today?"

"I'm a little concerned about Mikey," she answered.

"In what way?" Sean instantly asked.

"I'm concerned about the way Rachel and Liang have been treating him," Beth responded calmly.

61

"How do you mean?" Sean enquired. Surprised.

"I have tried to keep quiet about it, as I don't really work in that department," Beth began, "Though, the way they go out for cigarette breaks and leave him on his own for long periods of time is not right. When I was working in the back with them last week, Mikey and myself did most of the work. Mikey tried to continue his training of Liang, though was constantly interrupted by Rachel. I feel she was undermining him on purpose. It got to the stage where they began to ignore him completely. I noticed Mikey was extremely down yesterday and I feel that is the reason why. I believe it is the reason he is not in today and we need to help him, not punish him," she calmly informed her audience.

"That is not really the feedback we have had from your other colleagues, Beth," Sean contested.

"I am giving you, my feedback," Beth shot back, strongly.

"I thank you for it and I will be in touch if I need anything further from you," Sean nodded to her. Stretching his arm out to show her where the door was.

Beth gave a quizzical look to both, as she rose to leave.

"I don't think we need to bother with Liang's feedback," Sean announced to Siobhan. After Beth had left. "What do you make of it?" he asked.

"I think it is pretty much what we thought this morning," Siobhan replied. "He has slacked off in the training with the new starter. I feel it is more like he can't be bothered, than being incapable. He has got a bit of intelligence about him, so is surely capable of training somebody how to do a job he has done for eighteen months. I'm not sure what Beth's comments were all about? I know he is the one who sent them off for extra breaks. Bearing in mind, he has a reputation for taking longer breaks than anybody else. I think maybe, Beth and Mikey have a thing for each other and that's the reason she's sticking up for him."

"It appears that is the case," Sean agreed. "Thank you, Siobhan. After that, I need a bit of fresh air. I'm going for one of those breaks the little prick is so fond of," Sean joked getting up to leave his office.

When he had been outside the shop for a minute or so; Mr Jefferson came out, clutching a vinyl record he had just purchased.

"Hi, Sean," he greeted Sean's back.

Sean turned and spoke. "Hi, Mr Jefferson. New purchase?"

"Yes, one I've been after for a while." Mr Jefferson responded warmly.

"I'm glad we have been of service again. You're a valued customer of ours." Sean smiled at him.

"No surprise that Mikey isn't in today, is it?" Mr Jefferson asked. Quickly changing the subject.

"What makes you say that?" Sean responded. The question taking him by complete surprise.

"I saw him after he finished here, yesterday. Near his flat. Looked terrible. Really ill and worn down. I could clearly tell he had a virus of some sort, so I walked him back to his flat and told him he needs to get some medicine from the chemist," Mr Jefferson lied. "He told me he would be fine and just needed some sleep. I told him if he doesn't feel better today, then he needs to see the doctor. Is that where he's gone today?" Mr Jefferson asked.

"I don't think so," Sean replied. "I think he's just resting at home."

"Well, nobody listens to the advice of an old fool, do they?" Mr Jefferson heartily joked. "You will be my age one day, Seany!" he bellowed, clapping Sean on the shoulder.

"I hope to be as wise." Sean complimented.

"I bet you've missed him today?" Mr Jefferson quickly jumped in. Bringing the conversation back to where he wanted it. "He's your best worker. Works harder than anybody else. Always has to take the extra slack from that bone idle one in the back that he works with and that new starter, not made my mind up about him yet," he spoke. Perfectly putting his point across.

"I do pay attention to everything and have my way of dealing with things." Sean smiled back, coldly. "Now, if you excuse me. I need to get back up to work."

"Of course, no rest for the wicked." Mr Jefferson laughed and walked away.

It was five minutes to nine when Mikey eventually stirred from his slumber that morning. Instantly his heart started to palpitate, when he realised, he had slept through his alarm. "No! No! No! You fucking idiot! What have you done?"

He immediately grabbed his mobile and called Sean, to say he was sick and wouldn't be able to make it into work. "Ok. We will speak tomorrow," was all he got from him, before he hung up. He felt awful. Feelings of guilt overwhelmed his whole being. "What did I think I could have achieved by going out and getting smashed?" Were the thoughts running through his mind. "I just wanted a drink and hopefully, a bit of company. I got that didn't I?"

Looking back on it as he lay in bed, he realised that last night he felt the best he had in his whole adult life. His whole life maybe? For that matter. Mr Jefferson, or who? Yes, that's it. He said to call him Tom. Tom had been great company. In his hungover state, with his head a pounding drum of a headache, he recalled that Tom had given him great advice about work and life.

"Oh, but why did I have to tell him about my childhood? I never tell anybody about that. Never! What will he think of me now? He said I was strong to come through it. Though, he may secretly think less of me. He didn't seem too though, did he? He seemed to warm to me more after I told him about it. Why would he though? What would he gain out of it?"

Mikey realised that most of the people he had met before, only took an interest or did something for him, if they thought they could gain something out of it. Save a few exceptions. "Maybe Tom is one of those exceptions? What could he possibly gain out of me? Discount at the store? No, he gets that anyway now. Given the number of records he buys. Nothing." Was what he concluded. "He is just a genuine old man, that saw a weak young man in a pub and chose to spend his time trying to help him and make him a better person."

He remembered that last night he was so happy when he arrived back home and was even singing. What was he singing? The Cheese 'n' Chive song. He remembered he had not sung that since his childhood days. That was his happy song, wasn't it? He used to sing it when he was out playing in his happy place. Last night he was happy, wasn't he? When he was young, he used to spoil everything by getting dirty. He would go too far with his games and become the dirty boy that he hated. Last night he went too far as well. He got too drunk. "Now, I'm a dirty man because I didn't get up for work. Will I ever learn? It was not intentional. But I need to learn to control myself. There's a balloon in my mind, that pops every time I shine. Because I take things too far." He thought.

He woke again just after two thirty in the afternoon and his thoughts had turned to what he was going to say to Sean tomorrow. He thought he can't possibly tell him that he got drunk with his best customer and had a hangover. But, what if Mr Jefferson; or Tom, told Sean what transpired? "No. He wouldn't do that. I just know that he wouldn't." He quickly discounted that as a possibility.

Tariq though? He had told Tariq he was going to have some beers. Would he keep it to himself? If questioned, he would have to tell Sean. He could always deny it. Say, he changed his mind because he didn't feel well. That's plausible. What if he has told others about it, though? "Beth? No. Definitely no. She would never grass me up.

Rachel? I doubt it. She would protect me. Liang? He would. But surely, they would believe me over somebody who has worked there for a week. My word surely means more. I will just say I was ill today and if questioned about the couple of beers, I will say I changed my mind and went home, because I didn't feel well." He concluded. "I should be safe."

Sean Meltzer sat in front of the open fire in the living room of his Altrincham home, with a glass of his favourite single malt Scotch Whisky in his right hand. His wife and child; all that he loved in the world apart from his business, safely tucked up in bed. He was thinking about what to do with his employee, Mikey Wainwright.

When he had first interviewed him for the position, some eighteen months ago now. His first impressions were that he was extremely shy, though could see a huge amount of intelligence and potential in him. He decided to offer him the position in the back of the store that he had applied for. He had hoped that he would come out of himself more as time went on. He even thought that further down the line, he could have been a potential replacement for Siobhan. When she came to retire.

Things had not worked out that way, however. He had not kicked on in the way he had hoped. He was still the insular, shy person who had walked through the door to begin with. That disappointed him. He decided it was a lack of interest and ambition. Something which he could not tolerate. Given his attendance record, thoughts about his future had crossed his mind before. He had so far decided to keep him; as even with this and some worrying feedback from Siobhan, he knew he was competent at his job. He still hoped he would kick on and become the employee he thought he had. Now, he had this issue of today's absence. After the negative feedback he had from his colleagues; save Beth, which he put down to her just trying to stick up for him. For whatever reason. He wasn't all that interested in that. Following this, he was ready to pull the plug and have the conversation in the morning, to terminate his employment. Though, Mr Jefferson changed his mind. It cast doubt on the truth of the situation. He didn't doubt the feedback from Rachel and Tariq was correct, as far as they knew. What happened after he left work that day? Mr Jefferson has hardly any dealings with Mikey, so there is absolutely no reason why he would have lied. He believed what he had told him. So, on that basis, he had decided there was too much doubt to go through with the decision to terminate his employment. He decided that he would not make a big deal of it tomorrow and just ask him if he felt better. Then keep a more watchful eye on the situation.

Chapter 9

Mikey rose with his seven thirty alarm that morning. He pushed his covers down and sat up in his bed, pulled his knees up to his chin and hugged himself around them. He thought desperately. "Please, let everything be all right today. I have learnt my lesson. I won't go drinking again if everything will just be all right." His eyes, pleading with the open space in front of him. "What? Ever again?" he asked himself. "Well, maybe not. As I did enjoy myself. But definitely not when I have work the next day," he concluded.

He hated his walk to work and took his time getting there, as he dreaded his arrival and what might happen. The shutters were already up when he got there. Which meant that somebody was inside. He hoped upon all hope, it was not Sean or Siobhan waiting for him. It was Tariq. His heartbeat slowed a dozen paces when he realised; when he quickly scanned the place, that it was only Tariq present.

"Mikey, you little rascal," he greeted him, laughing a warm laugh. "Listen mate. I covered for you the best I could yesterday. I made some shit up about not knowing when you were going for a beer. I said I thought you said at the weekend. Somehow Sean knew we had that conversation. I don't know how, but he knew. Eyes and ears everywhere that fella. Listen, I winged it as best as I could, so just play it cool mate and you'll be all right," Tariq assured him. With a more serious tone to his voice now.

"Cheers, Tariq. I really appreciate that. It means a lot."

Mikey genuinely thanked him. "But I decided against it anyway." He lied. He decided that keeping the same story for everybody would be the best way forward and surprised himself with how easily the notion came to him. "Maybe I am learning," he thought. What was it that Tom said? "Sometimes, you just have to pretend." He couldn't have put it better himself.

"Ok mate. Are you feeling better now?" Tariq enquired with concern.

"A little. Not 100%, but better." Mikey replied. Which was the truth. He had recovered sufficiently from his hangover, though it still lingered somewhat.

"Good," Tariq announced. "Just take it easy today, the best you can." He smiled before turning his attention to the paperwork on the front desk.

Mikey walked into the kitchen, made himself a coffee from the machine and went to sit at his desk and fire up his waiting laptop. As he sat there on his own for the next few minutes, he pondered whether it was okay that he just lied to Tariq? He had covered for him when he didn't need to and had been repaid with a lie. After deliberating this, he concluded that it was all right. He had been intending to tell everybody that he hadn't gone for a beer anyway. So, telling Tariq a little white lie, was acceptable. He would never be hurt by it. If he never found out the truth.

"What a naughty boy you've been," was how Rachel entered the room with Liang in tow.

Mikey looked up at her. Trying with all his might, to look as confused by her statement as possible.

"Don't pull the innocent with me," she teased. "I know you went out and got smashed the other night. You don't have to lie to me, Mikey."

"I, I didn't." Mikey stammered. "I went home sick," he

announced. Sticking to the lie as best he could.

"Well, you can stick to your story if you want. But we all know the truth," Rachel announced with a side glance to Liang.

"You can't fool us," he spoke. Joining in the conversation. "We know what you were up to and so does Sean and Siobhan. I wouldn't want to be in your shoes today." Liang laughed. His six-foot five frame towering over Mikey.

Mikey could feel himself getting hot under the collar and felt the sweat beginning to drip from every pore. He was feverishly trying to think of a response, but none was forthcoming. Until he eventually managed. "You can think what you like."

"Whatever," Liang nonchalantly fired back. Before turning to Rachel. "Quick cig before we start?"

"Why not?" was her simple response.

As they both left the room, Mikey put his fingers under his laptop to move it a bit closer and came across a folded piece of paper. After glancing round to see if anybody was watching and realising, they weren't he opened it.

'Mikey, I hope you're okay? Please stay strong and talk to me if things get too much. Beth X'

He slid the note into his jeans. Workwear at Energy Records was always smart-casual. Unless there were important visitors attending. Which was rare. He was petrified by what Rachel and Liang had said to him. What if Sean and Siobhan did know? Then he was in danger and how could he keep his lie up? If they really did know. They would not believe him and see straight through any story he told. Beth's note had calmed him somewhat, though. "Such a nice thing to do," he thought. Then quickly turning to face his screen to start working when his two colleagues came back into the room.

He worked in silence for the next half an hour or so. Vaguely listening to Rachel and Liangs conversation. Which he found nonsensical and boring if he was honest. Then he heard both Sean and Siobhan greeting Tariq and Beth at the front desk. Then, footsteps heading towards the back room. He stared harder at his computer screen. Hoping they might just go away if they saw him busy working.

"Good morning," Sean's voice to the room upon entering.

"Good morning," was everybody's reply. With Mikey's a lot less audible than the other two.

"Are you feeling better today, Mikey?" Sean asked.

"A little. Not 100%, but better," he answered, repeating what he had told Tariq. Barely looking up at Sean as he spoke.

"Good." Sean nodded. "If the day goes on and you feel unwell. Come and find me and I will send you home. If you feel up to staying? Then have a good day," he assured him before turning to leave the room.

After he had gone and was well and truly out of earshot. Rachel turned to him and viciously said. "You're a fucking cat with nine lives you!" Before stomping off into the kitchen.

Mikey was perplexed. Why had she just spoken to him like that? Surely, she would have been happy that he had seemingly got a reprieve. And how did she know that he was planning to go for a drink? He couldn't work it out. It was all terribly confusing for him. He worked in silence and lost in his own thoughts for the rest of the morning. Save for when Siobhan entered the room to speak with Rachel. She barely even gave Mikey a second glance, though his heart rate went through the roof upon seeing her. She was just very cold and dismissive of him. Treating him like she wasn't even aware of his presence.

Beth left the shop for an hour just before 3pm, to attend a routine dental appointment and with not much going on at the front desk; Tariq joined his remaining colleagues in the back. If for no other reason than to cure his boredom.

"How's everybody doing back here?" he asked. "Dead to the world out there."

"Pretty quiet here, too," Liang sighed.

Tariq nodded and asked Mikey. "You feel all right, still?"

"There's nothing wrong with him, Tariq. For God's sake," Rachel flew in. Before Mikey had chance to reply.

"Guys been ill," Tariq responded.

"Ill?" Rachel flippantly retorted. "Hungover more like."

"Nah…" Tariq started.

"You said he was going out to sink ten pints!" she asserted. her voice rising.

"I said he was thinking about having a couple," Tariq shot back. His voice also beginning to rise.

"I can't believe Sean only asked him how he was feeling," she condemned.

"You fucking grassed on him, didn't you?" he accused.

"No! No, I didn't. I swear."

"You fucking did, you snake."

"I just told the truth."

"I thought you were better than that."

"I didn't say anything. Just said what I knew."

"Unbelievable!"

"It's all right. Sean knows he was ill. We stick together as a team."

"Team and a fucking snake."

Just then, the front door of the shop opened, and a customer appeared. A short man, around fifty waiting for service. Tariq glared at Rachel before making his way to the front desk.

"I didn't Mikey, I swear," Rachel pleaded when Tariq left the

72

room. Quietly now, as not to let the customer hear.

Mikey had never seen Rachel so agitated and didn't know what to make of it. His hands were shaking at this point, and he folded them to not let on. "Surely, it can't be true?" he thought. "But what if it is? No, it can't be," he reiterated to himself. Why had Tariq told Rachel though? Was that innocent? He didn't know. He could feel himself sweating. He didn't know what to make of any of it. It must be just some big misunderstanding. She couldn't have meant any real harm. But, what about the cat with nine lives comment? No. She was joking. He saw her stomp away, shaking her head, laughing. It was a misunderstanding and Rachel, and Tariq would sort it out between themselves. What had he done? It was all his fault. If he hadn't had been so stupid as to get drunk, none of this would have happened. He had to make it all right. "It's okay, Rachel. Everything will work out," he said out loud by way of reassuring her.

"I would never hurt you, Mikey," Rachel croaked. Sobbing a little.

"We will work it out with Tariq," Mikey promised.

"Thank you," Rachel replied, looking crestfallen.

Tariq stayed at the front of the shop for the rest of the afternoon and as time went by, Rachel became more of her old self. She was laughing and joking with Mikey by the end of the day. Teasing him that a good-looking guy like him, should get himself a girlfriend. She said that girls would claw each other's eyes out to get to him.

Strangely, Mikey felt better about his relationship with her than he had in a good while. They got on swimmingly. Just like they had in the past; at times when it was just the two of them. Liang seemed like an afterthought to her.

When they were locking the shop up at the close of business,

Tariq instantly turned to him and spoke. "Mikey, listen. I only told Rachel about what you said as a joke. I didn't think it would go any further. I'm sorry, man. I thought I could trust her."

"It's okay, Tariq. I believe you," Mikey reassured. And he actually did believe him. There was something in his mannerisms and tone, that smelt of the truth. "I just want you and Rachel to be okay with each other. I don't think she would have grassed me up on purpose."

"I hope you're right, mate." Tariq slowly stated. "I'm just not convinced. I hope I'm wrong. Maybe, just see how it plays out? Are we good?"

"Yeah, we're good." Mikey confirmed. "Until tomorrow, then."

"See you tomorrow."

"And Mikey. Be good tonight." Tariq winked and smiled. Before walking on home.

Mikey was numb to confusion all the way home. He didn't know what to make of the day's events. When he got into his flat, he sat on his couch and did something he hadn't done in quite some time. He put his thoughts to paper. He wrote,

What about me upsets you? What makes your anger swell?

Through the dwell of your lazy eye? For I am much more than you see Always tried to fit my jigsaw piece Though never found one that fits Deserted, long and winding streets A momentary lapse in my condition

I found the strength of love condense That flicker of a most beautiful second Before reality bites and beckons

To the dark secluded measures That somehow bring such pleasures

For only the weary traveller could level Where the storm ceases hope forever Treasures seldom seen on a night so lean Just to feel a gentle gleam of self-esteem The dream somehow to be embraced

A gentle light in a haze of fearful fright A star to be born and burn so bright

But how? To summon the will of its might Cascade through shade with courage engaged

Ritual of habitual wanting of belonging, not displayed As a place is found to rest the exhausted head

Where sunrise looms, the flower does bloom Raging excitement, bellows a new day dawning Restoring the leaves of shattered trees

What about me upsets me?

My awakening never reaching full bloom.

His head swam dizzy after he set the pen to rest. Though his hands did not tremble.

Chapter 10

Mikey found the time over the remainder of the week, to thank Beth for her note. He assured her that he was feeling much better about things and the dynamic in the back room was now more to his liking. He was talking more with Rachel again and had even had a few chats with Liang. He was more pleasant than he had been and although their conversations were not too in depth. He sensed an overall change in working relations between them, that was for the better. Beth was delighted with this and told Mikey as much. She did; however, caution him to keep his wits about him and protect himself from any further harm. "What is it about people telling me to protect myself? First Tom and now Beth." He needed to work out what that was all about? He was both surprised and delighted, that he had managed to convey more of how he felt to Beth. The thing he loved the most, was how she had reacted. She had exuded joy at the news and budded him to keep going from strength to strength. "She's so smart and caring." He smiled to himself.

When the working week ended and he had locked up with and said his usual goodbye to Tariq, he found himself walking with a spring in his step. He knew exactly where he was heading, The Old White Lion. He wanted to see Tom. He was concerned about his absence from the shop. He had not seen him come in all week. Had he said something that might have upset him? When they had a drink together? He didn't think so. He in fact, knew he hadn't. Though his mind always played these tricks on him and made him second guess himself. He knew that it was concern for Tom that he was feeling. He needed to make sure nothing had happened to him. As after all, he was getting on in years now and it was unusual for him not to come into the shop for a whole week. Even if he only came in for 'a perusal'. As the old man described it. He always came in at least once a week. Mikey quickened his step, anxious to reach his destination. He was still incredibly nervous about going in, though he managed to steel himself a little more this time. He did so by concentrating on the fact that he was going there, in the hope of meeting somebody he knew he would.

Mr Jefferson had seated himself at the bar and was reading *The Guardian* newspaper when Mikey arrived.

"Mikey!!!" He joyfully enthused upon seeing him enter. "Hi, Mr…erm Tom." Mikey stumbled his reply.

"Just finished work?" Mr Jefferson asked.

"Yeah, done for the week," Mikey announced. Noticing the barmaid approaching.

"Well, time for a drink then," Mr Jefferson announced. Turning to face the young lady, working behind the bar. Mikey noticed that it wasn't Sue today. It was somebody younger. Perhaps in her mid-twenties, he figured. "Same again for me please, Tanya. And a pint of Carlsberg for my companion here." Mr Jefferson made their order.

Tanya came back with the drinks and Mr Jefferson paid. Upon receiving his change and Tanya saying, "Thank you." Mikey noticed her smile at him and make eye contact. Which made him feel both elated and incredibly nervous at the same time. With her dark eyes melting into his, for just a glimmer of a second.

"Come on. Our seats are free. Let's sit down," Mr Jefferson

instructed. Already beginning to move towards the seats they took when they were last in the establishment.

"Good to see you in here again, Mikey." Mr Jefferson began. When they were seated. "I was beginning to think I'd scared you off." He laughed.

"Not at all." Mikey dully replied. "I was just saving my next drink for the weekend."

"And now, it is upon us. Cheers!" Mr Jefferson spoke back. Clinking his glass with Mikey's. His natural northeast accent becoming more prominent.

Mikey smiled a hearty grin back and responded. "Cheers."

"Have you missed me at the shop?" Mr Jefferson then asked.

"Yeah. I've noticed you've not been in all week." Mikey eagerly replied. Knowing this is what he came in for.

"Good to see an old man is still missed." Mr Jefferson grinned. "Just had a few errands to run is all. Nothing troubling. Just things that needed taking care of. So, set your mind to rest on that young man," he explained. Sensing his compatriot was looking for an explanation. This warmed him. Inwardly, he had hoped Mikey would have been concerned as to why he hadn't been in when he thought about it during the days that had passed.

"I'm glad to hear it," Mikey announced.

Mr Jefferson thought about his next question for a moment. As, he knew the different possibilities by way of answer. Given the fact that he also knew of Mikey's absence from work. The day after they last met. He asked. "How are things going at work?"

At first, he clammed up after hearing the question. Then told himself that Tom deserved a proper answer. He had been kind and given him great advice when there was no need to do so. He also, quickly grasped that he shouldn't mention that he took the day off work after their previous encounter. He thought this would only hurt his feelings. He confided. "Things are much better now. I'm even talking with Liang." He laughed. "Was that a joke?" He thought to himself.

"Good to hear," Mr Jefferson chipped in. Then immediately fell silent. To give Mikey the space to continue.

"I feel I have made real progress," Mikey continued. "I don't feel as anxious all the time. I'm still on edge most of the time, but I feel I'm learning to control it better. I'm learning to pretend. I'm beginning to think that all I must do, is give off better signals. I don't know how to do that yet. Is that what people do? They pretend they're all right in front of others. Then, work out how to make themselves better when they're alone."

"There is truth in that, yes," Mr Jefferson pondered. "Although, that only takes you so far. Pretending can get you some of the way. But sooner or later, if you continue down that path. You will get found out. People are more perceptive than they let on and, more than they even know themselves. So, it is the first step. Whilst you're climbing the first rung of that ladder, you must learn how to make that person you want to be, a reality. As when the time comes when you must, you will be ready."

Mikey listened deep in thought and after several moments, replied. "I'm not sure who I want to be? All I know, is I want to be better than I am now."

"You already are," Mr Jefferson complimented. "When I saw you for the first time in here, I could see how nervous you were. Your hand was shaking holding your pint.

Today, however, much less so. You entered with a little more confidence. With each passing day, just make yourself a little better than you were the previous day and, the rest will naturally follow."

"How do I do that?" Mikey asked intently.

"When you are alone at night, think of one thing you didn't do so well that day," Mr Jefferson answered. "Don't beat yourself up about it," he continued. "Just think how you can improve next time. Do you make your bed when you get out of it in the morning?" he asked.

A bit flummoxed by the question, Mikey simply replied. "No."

"Tomorrow. I want you to," Mr Jefferson instructed. "Then the next day, something else. Before you know it, you will have a natural orderly routine, that you can feel good about. This in turn, will make you feel better about yourself." He spoke softly. Then chirped, "Speaking of turns, it's your round."

Mikey smiled and rose to walk to the bar. He was warmly greeted by Tanya, who took his order of a Carlsberg and John Smiths. When she returned and gave him his change, she spoke. "I haven't seen you in here before."

"Only the second time I've been in," was Mikey's fumbling reply.

"Where do you normally go?" Tanya asked.

"I, I don't really," Mikey stammered.

"Well, I work here on Saturday afternoons and Sunday nights," Tanya informed him, smiling.

"Ok," Mikey mumbled. Not knowing what to say next. He just gave back a quick shy smile, then turned to head back to his table. Feeling the sweat drip down his back.

"Chalk one up for the underdogs," was how Mr Jefferson greeted him. Mikey gave back a puzzled look, reseating himself.

"You and me are both underdogs," Mr Jefferson told him. "We are more similar than you think."

"I don't think so," Mikey countered.

"That girl behind the bar has taken a shine to you," he enlightened him.

"She was just being friendly. It's her job," Mikey noted.

"It was more than that. It seems the lesson for today, is learning to read female signals. They send them out to us in some sort of morse code and, it's up to us to work them out," Mr Jefferson taught his drinking buddy.

"I don't know how," Mikey replied. Feeling ashamed.

"I am sixty years old and I'm still trying," Mr Jefferson laughed. "So don't feel embarrassed or anything. Women are much more complex than us. Pleasing them takes practice. You're of an age where marriage and a family are still possible for you. Whereas me, I'm too old."

"Have you ever married and had children? May I ask?" Mikey carefully questioned.

"By all means you can ask," Mr Jefferson answered. A furrowed brow came across his features then and, he looked at Mikey intently for a long moment. Before eventually answering. "I never got round to it. Too busy being a rascal up in Darlington. I had more than my fair share of women. But never got around to taking one to wed. I wanted to with one, once. But she was with another man. I'm not proud of the fact that we had an affair behind his back."

"What happened?" Mikey quietly asked.

"He found out. Went ballistic. As you would imagine," Mr Jefferson informed. All joy slipping from his face. "They ended up getting into a huge fight and she ended up banging his head against the wall, as he held her by the throat. Killed him. The impact was directly on the temple, you see," he slowly and thoughtfully relayed.

"That's a terrible thing to happen," Mikey responded. "But

you shouldn't blame yourself. You were young and you could have had no way of knowing it would end like that."

"Promise me something," Mr Jefferson beckoned. Mikey nodded.

"If you get the opportunity to have a family with somebody you love, I want you to grasp it," Mr Jefferson said with more intensity in him than Mikey had ever seen before. "Whether that is with the pretty girl behind this bar, or anybody else. I want you to give everything you have for it. Make the time and cherish every moment you have with them. As, not everybody is that lucky."

"I will," Mikey promised. "But I don't think I am one of the lucky ones."

"Like I said. You and me are more similar than you know." Mr Jefferson leaned in closer. "We're both underdogs. I had a troubled childhood, just like you. I had to fight to get everything, the same as you. This can be turned to our advantage. As nobody will see us coming and will underestimate us. That's what gives us our edge."

Mikey was dumbfounded and just stared at Mr Jefferson.

The tension was interrupted by Tanya saying goodbye to the patrons of the pub, as she was ending her shift. She waved to Mr Jefferson and smiled to Mikey. "See you?"

Mikey nodded and she smiled and left. "See," Mr Jefferson teased. "Better already."

They left the pub upon finishing their drinks, as Mr Jefferson wanted to go home to eat. He told Mikey it was traditional for him to have fish 'n' chips from the chippy on a Saturday evening. They wished each other a good night and went their separate ways.

As Mikey was walking up the stairs to his apartment, Colin came in behind him and shouted up. "Hey, Mikey! How you doing?"

"I'm good. How are you?" Mikey replied. Instantly feeling the dread of bumping into him as soon as he heard the communal door open.

"What you doing tonight?" Colin excitedly asked.

"Just, just going to chill," Mikey stumbled.

"No, you're not!" Colin announced. Grinning and clapping Mikey on the shoulder. "You're coming out with me."

"I've already had a few in the White Lion, though," Mikey tried to excuse himself.

"Even better," Colin concluded. "It means you're already warmed up for tonight. Listen, I'm going to grab a quick shower. So, I will knock on for you in about twenty minutes. Don't let me down now," He almost demanded of his neighbour. Embracing Mikey's hand into his.

"Okay," was all Mikey could manage before Colin sauntered into his apartment, singing to himself.

Mikey couldn't fathom what just happened, as he made his way into his own apartment. He had no intention of going out for a drink with Colin. But he had somehow just agreed to it. He couldn't back out now. He would be knocking on the door in less than twenty minutes. He thought. "I may as well have a shower myself."

Mikey and Colin entered the street twenty-five minutes later and walked left down the road. Turning left just before the library. "Where are we going?" Mikey asked. Feeling anxious about the situation.

"I reckon, a couple in the Knowsley. Then onto Lloyds for some shenanigans." Colin grinned back. As they approached the entrance for the pub at the end of the street.

Mikey just nodded and followed him into the establishment. His eyes searching the place frantically, with a mixture of nervousness and excitement.

"What you having, Mikey?" Colin asked. When they reached the bar. "Carlsberg, please," Mikey mumbled back.

"Good choice." Colin asserted. "Two pints of Carlsberg," he said to the approaching bar man.

They got their drinks and found seats around the corner, near the pool table. Mikey was holding himself together, listening to Colin's inane conversation about the ladies, or 'talent' as he referred to them. That was in the place. Of how he would fuck her senseless. Or smash another all night. He bragged at length about the women he'd slept with and all the 'Booty calls' he had in his phone.

When Mikey had bought the second round of drinks and made his way back to the table. He noticed Colin coming back from the smoking area with his phone in hand. He wasn't aware that he smoked. Although granted, he had never socialised with him before. "I've just ordered us some goodies. He will be here in ten," he announced reseating himself.

"What on Earth is he talking about?" Mikey thought in his head. "Goodies. What can that mean? And who will be here in ten minutes?" He thought it best to keep all this to himself, as he didn't want to appear stupid. So, he just nodded and spoke, "Ok."

Colin seemed agitated for the next fifteen minutes or so, constantly checking his phone. Before it finally rang, and he made his way outside. Without even so much as a look in Mikey's direction. "Should I follow him?" Mikey thought. He decided against it and took a sip of his beer.

Colin arrived back a couple of minutes later and spoke.

"Follow me up to the toilets in a minute. I will be in the left cubicle." He got up to leave at such speed, it gave Mikey no chance to respond.

To reach the male toilets, you had to climb stairs with two sections, which doubled back on each other. Mikey did so and walked down the short corridor to the toilets and entered. Nobody was in there. He nervously tried to open the left cubicle door, to suddenly find it opened and ushered inside by Colin who had a small key in his hand, with some white powder on the end of it. Mikey realised what it was. "Quickly," Colin told him.

Mikey sniffed the powder up his nose. He knew this was against his better judgement, but he felt compelled to do so. He had never done cocaine before. In fact, he had never so much as even smoked a cigarette in his life. He didn't really want to do it. Though he thought he would look stupid in front of Colin if he refused. Colin quickly beckoned him out of the cubicle and instructed. "You wash your hands and leave it a minute, before you come down."

Mikey did as he was bid. Feeling a sensation come over him, that he had never experienced before. A massive rush to his head. He felt his mouth tingle, as he sniffed the remaining powder up his nose and found it entering his throat, into his mouth. As he descended the stairs, he felt like he was flying. The world felt like a different place. He sailed back to the table, where he found Colin who grinned and asked. "Good shit, yeah?"

"Yeah," was all Mikey could manage.

"Drink up." Colin instructed. "I want to get another round and hit in before we move on. We don't have to pay to get into Lloyds if we get there before ten," he announced further, leaving the table and heading to the bar.

Mikey did so. The beer going down more freely than it had

before. When they both had fresh pints in front of them, he suddenly felt compelled to talk. A strange feeling for him. "What do you do for a living?" he asked.

"Painter and decorator," Colin answered. "Been on at the estate agents to let me redo the hall and landing in our place. Like usual, they're not interested. Just want your money."

"Yeah, they do. Still not fixed the light in the hall, the dicks." Mikey joked. Feeling like he could talk for a lot longer. "There's lots of things in that place that need seeing to. Fucking door handles in my place are all loose. And that banister on the stairs. Only a matter of time before that falls over."

"One bump and he's come out of himself," Colin interrupted. "Talking for England. I've not heard you utter two words to me before and now I can't shut you up."

Mikey knew he was feeling more adrenaline than he had ever felt before. He had a rush of energy that was beginning to overwhelm him. He thought, "This is the best feeling in the world." Before replying to his companion. "Just feeling a buzz. I've never felt so alive before. I've always wanted to talk to you. But never really had the chance. We only ever see each other passing in the corridor, or on the stairs. Not great for conversation. I'm glad we've got this chance now, though, I've always thought you were a great guy and have wanted to know you better," Mikey explained. The words seemingly running like water now. A new feeling for him. One which he enjoyed.

"Have you ever done sniff before?" Colin asked.

Mikey thought to lie and say he had. Though, something told him that Colin would know if he did. He said instead, "No. I've always wanted to try it. But never got the chance."

"Now you have." Colin laughed. "Take it easy tonight, as its your first time. Take this, have another hit in the cubicle and bring it back down for me," he instructed.

Handing Mikey the bag with the small key under the table. Mikey did so.

They left after finishing their drinks to head to Lloyds. Which had now become the primary place to drink and dance, since the Sol Viva night club had closed. To make way for The Rock shopping complex, which Energy Records was situated right next door to. Being directly across from the bus and Metrolink stations. It makes for easy access to revellers from all areas.

They joined the back of the queue to enter, when a couple of young ladies joined behind them. Noticing as much, Colin turned to the one directly behind him with curly blonde hair and spoke. "Let you go in front of us if I can have a dance?"

"No thanks, creep," she dismissed him. Turning her face back to her tall blonde companion.

Both Mikey and Colin laughed at this and were let in easily by the two bouncers on the front door. The ladies behind were not so lucky. As is always the case in such places, they were asked to provide ID. Which they did and gained entry.

After another pint and hit of cocaine, Mikey suddenly found himself on the dance floor. Beckoned there by Colin. He felt on top of the world and tried his best to pull off some moves, even though he clearly had two left feet. He even tried to speak to a pretty black girl, who was enjoying herself with some friends. Though his mouth was running away with itself by now and she struggled to understand what he was saying. The loud dance music not helping his cause. She finally gave up and smiled. Before walking back to her friends. Purposely turning her back on Mikey.

Colin himself, had no luck with the ladies try as he did.

Noticing this, Mikey said in his ear. "Come on, mate. You always get the ladies. Help us get lucky."

"I'm just getting warmed up, mate. Don't worry," Colin reassured. Moving to try his luck with another unsuspecting female.

They ended their time in Lloyds with a few more drinks and hits. With no luck with the opposite sex. Colin said he was going to score another fifty bag and head round to his mate's house. He asked if Mikey wanted to join. Mikey declined as his head felt all over the place. He strangely didn't feel all that drunk. Even though he had consumed quite a bit of alcohol. They hugged each other outside and went their separate ways.

Mikey headed back to his flat and upon reaching it, didn't feel like going to sleep. He instead put the first Spark Town album on his headphones and sung along. He knew all the words. He much preferred this album, as it had Tony playing the bass. He remembered his conversation with Siobhan about the new bass player and concluded that he should have just told her that Tony was much better. He needed to be more forthright. Like he had been tonight. His head swam with a mixture of euphoria and delirium as he listened to the eleven-track debut album. After which, he decided that sleep would be a good course of action.

Sleep did not come easy to him that night. No matter how hard he tried, he just couldn't set his mind to rest. Thoughts of the day's events swirled through him like hurricanes, and he couldn't shut them up. He left the comfort of his bed to urinate several times and he thought. "What the hell is wrong with me?" It was just after 4am when sleep finally prevailed.

He did not rise from his slumber until past 4pm that Sunday afternoon. Save for getting up to relieve his bladder in the bathroom. Every time he rose, his nose felt like it was full of cement, and he was constantly blowing it. When he did climb out of bed and tried to recall the events of the previous evening, they strangely came back to him more vividly than the previous time he had been hungover. He recalled everything that happened in the pub with Tom and the story he had told. Mikey instantly hoped he was okay. As it was a graphic tale and one, he was not expecting. It was desperately sad. He wondered how Tom could be such a jovial, fun guy. Knowing what had transpired all those years ago. Near on thirty years in fact. What was it he said? "Sometimes, you just have to pretend." Maybe he pretends he's okay. Though, it eats him up inside. He could tell with how intently he had told the story, that it has affected his life ever since. Now, he goes about putting on a front, acting like he hasn't got a care in the world. When really, he must be beat up about what happened. Mikey thought he should do the same about his past. He said out loud. "How amazing would it be, if I never thought about the bad thing again?"

He then recalled his time with Colin. "What the fuck?" He thought. "Why did I have to see him on my way home? I didn't want to go out with him. He practically forced me, and I just knew he wouldn't have taken no for an answer. And shit, I took cocaine.

Again, I never wanted to. He just handed it to me, and I felt obliged. I could have hardly refused, could I? Then I was talking. Talking like a bumbling idiot to him and anybody else that would listen to me. Is that what that stuff does to you? I don't want any more if that's the case. Why did I have to tell him that I'd always wanted to talk to him? I never have. Truth is, I dread seeing him. A feeling of dread comes all over me whenever I see him. But last night I enjoyed it." He had to admit that. He had enjoyed

Colin's company and the fact that for the first time in his adult life, he was able to freely express himself. Even though he did jabber on nonsensically. He revelled in the fact that he communicated properly with people. He remembered even speaking to a girl. Even though that didn't get anywhere. As he was a bumbling buffoon. That was progress, wasn't it? Tom had said. "Just try to be better than you were yesterday." Upon recalling this, he instantly went back into his bedroom to make his bed.

Chapter 11

Mikey went back to bed that evening at around 8pm and slept the whole night through. He still felt groggy when he rose for work the next day. He remembered to make his bed as he got out of it. "How long until I make that a habit?" he thought. His nose felt like it was on fire when he was drinking his morning coffee. "Why did I have to put that shit up there?" he asked himself. "Colin," he concluded. He wondered how Colin dealt with these feelings. After all, he must have them all the time if he does it every weekend. He was about to leave his empty coffee cup in the sink, as usual before, he was suddenly compelled to rinse it. He did so and put it on the draining board. "Another step," he realised.

He felt strangely agitated that day in work. He'd had a good night's sleep, but he still felt tired. This had him on edge. So much so, that he spilt milk all over the kitchen top when making himself a coffee on his break. "Fuck sake!" he cursed.

"Who pissed on your chips?" Tariq chirped. Amused.

"Sorry, nobody. Just not a good night's sleep," Mikey apologised.

"It's all right, mate." Tariq reassured. "You should let your feelings out more. It's good for the soul."

"Anger surely isn't. Is it?" Mikey queried.

"In the right context, yes," Tariq taught. "Everybody gets angry. I used to have a real issue with it. Then, I bought myself one of those heavy punching bags that boxers use. I have been more chilled ever since. Started doing a bit of training and now, I'm even considering having some white-collar fights. Though, the missus is not happy about that."

"Doesn't like you training?" Mikey asked.

"Doesn't want me to fight. Scared these handsome features of mine will get filled in by some meat head." Tariq laughed.

"They won't if you're good," Mikey encouraged.

"That's what I tell her," Tariq announced. "I tell her that I'm too good to get hit. You should consider giving it a go. You might enjoy it."

"I'm not sure. I've never really had a fight in my life," Mikey declared. "You never know how good you are, unless you try." Tariq heartened.

"Try what?" Liang asked, entering to grab two bottles of water from the fridge. "Mikey here might be considering giving boxing a go," Tariq informed.

"Seriously?" Liang asked. With a screwed up, almost mocking face. "You have to be tough to do boxing."

"Who says I'm not?" Mikey stiffly asked. Surprising his audience and himself, even more so with this sudden outburst.

"Look at you," Liang answered, looking Mikey up and down. "There's nothing about you. You need to hit the gym before you even think about boxing. You will get broken in half if you don't."

Mikey felt a sudden rush of anger build up inside of himself. He really wanted to rebuff the insults. Though his mouth wouldn't open to speak. He saw Liang standing there, with a condescending grin on his face. But no words came forth. He knew he had to say something. He just couldn't. After several moments, Mikey left the room and went back to his desk.

There would be no respite there either. Siobhan was there,

sat in his chair. "Mikey. I need you to look at this order with me, please," she calmly told him, rising from the chair.

Mikey sat down and spoke, "Yes, sure." Feeling the sweat begin to surface again. He knew it must be a mistake.

"I have spoken with Rachel already about this, as it was in her inbox," Siobhan began. Giving a look to her. "Though, she assures me that it was you who did this. It is the very first order you did with Liang," she continued, looking flatly at him. "As you can see, the customer has sent us a complaint email. Two items were missing from his order."

"I, I can see that, yes," Mikey fumbled.

"It makes us look unprofessional," she firmly told him.

Mikey stayed silent. So, Siobhan continued. "What happened with it?" she asked.

It was then that he looked at the time the order was processed. It was 2:32 p.m. of the day he first let Liang process a few simple orders. His own email account hadn't been set up by then, so he was shadowing him before this time and... yes! Of course. It was Rachel's he used to start with when Beth came to help. It couldn't have been him. It must be Rachel that did it with Liang. What to do about it? Should he say something? It might get her into trouble if he did. How did she not know it was her that did it, though? She must remember. It was busy that day. So maybe she had forgotten. "I need to say something. But I need to do it in a way that doesn't get Rachel into trouble. I have to be careful here," he concluded in his head.

"I'm not sure it was me," he finally answered.

"Are you calling me a liar?" Rachel instantly jumped in.

"No...I..." He tailed off.

"Go on Mikey. This better be good." Siobhan beckoned. Motioning for silence from Rachel.

"I, I worked on orders with Liang in the morning only on that day," he started. Frantically trying to find the right words. "I only mean there may be a bit of confusion. Liang worked with Rachel for most of that afternoon and as it was his first order, perhaps he just made a mistake. Which is completely understandable.

Considering he hadn't done it before. We were busy that day and it looks like it just got overlooked, unfortunately." He prayed this would satisfy.

"You were in charge of this young man's training," Siobhan told him, pointing towards Liang. "The way I see it is, that you neglected that responsibility because you couldn't be bothered."

"No. I, I left him to work with Rachel as they worked well together and thought it best," he tried.

"Do be quiet! I'm not finished." Siobhan ordered. "I understand that it was a busy day. In my experience, days like that require added focus and concentration.

Something which you seem to lack. It was lazy, sloppy work. What amazes me the most, is that you have tried to pass it off onto somebody who has only been with us a short time. Furthermore, you have tried to drag Rachel down with you. That I will not stand for. She works hard for this company, and I will not have you tarnish her reputation. It is one thing to make a mistake. But then to try and cover up for yourself by blaming others, is very devious. I will not stand for that in my workplace. Take this as a severe warning as to your future conduct," she furiously spelled out to him.

"It was not him." A voice came from behind Siobhan. Beth stood in the doorway.

"Excuse me?" Siobhan asked her. Turning around.

"The order was for three vinyl records, a couple of posters

and two t shirts. Am I correct?" Beth enquired. With a calm assurance of her knowledge.

"How do you know that?" Siobhan responded. Surprised.

"Elephants ask me to remind them of things," Beth dismissively answered.

"Don't you get cheeky with me, young lady…" Siobhan flushed.

"That order was done when I was in the room myself," Beth interrupted, calmly. "If you look in Mikey's inbox. You will find that at the same time, there is a rather large order for a Mrs Thomas. Surprise 50th wedding anniversary gifts for her husband. I worked with him on this, as it was a lot to get together. It took us the best part of half an hour to get it ready. With having to box everything up and triple check we had everything. Considering the size and what it was for. I specifically remember Liang telling Rachel only saddos listen to Dire Straits. Which one of their LPs is part of the order in question. If I'm not mistaken? So, Mikey is correct in what he has told you."

"I'm not sure about this, Beth," responded Siobhan. Clearly irritated by what she had just heard.

"The evidence is all there," Beth told her.

"Don't you dare tell me how to do my job!" Siobhan viciously attacked.

"Mistakes happen when new starters come on board. It is part of the learning process," Beth informed her. "It is unfortunate, but these things happen. I don't see any more to it than that and pointing fingers will not resolve the issue."

"You have some nerve, young lady!" Siobhan was getting volatile by this point. Beth remained calm. "I will be speaking to Sean about this! We will see what he makes of your insolence!" she threatened Beth.

"I am happy that you will be doing so," Beth responded. "Then when everything has been cleared up. I'm sure you will be happy to furnish Mikey with the apology that he deserves." She innocently smiled. Using her features to full effect.

Siobhan glared at her.

Beth turned to look at Rachel and Liang to articulate her next words. "I am not trying to throw anybody under the bus here. We are a team, and we all make mistakes. We all need to look out for one another. I meant no offence to either of you. It was a hell of a busy day that day. You can't be expected to remember every order you did."

"That's enough from you!" Siobhan barked at her. "Time to get back to work."

Beth nonchalantly returned to the front desk and Siobhan pounded up the stairs, to Sean's office.

When they had both left. Rachel vacantly commented. "She thinks she knows it all, that one. She's getting too big for her boots."

"She is right," Mikey contested. Feeling the need to defend Beth.

"I know she was," Rachel conceded. "It's just the way she spoke to Siobhan and to think, she can accuse me of not knowing what I'm doing. I will be having words."

"I don't think you have any right to," Mikey told her. A bit abruptly. He didn't know why he had just spoken like that. But he knew it felt like the right thing.

"Excuse me!" Rachel demanded.

"I, I mean." He was stumbling again. "Control yourself," he demanded of himself. "She only said what was right. She wasn't trying to blame anybody. She was just sticking up for me, is all. She told you herself that we're a team and need to look out for one another. You didn't do anything wrong. You just couldn't remember that it wasn't me who did that order. You can't hold Beth having a good memory against her. It was Siobhan who was out of order if anything. For not finding out the truth, before having a go at me. She just stuck up for her work colleague." Mikey didn't know where the words were coming from. But it felt good.

"Haven't you got the balls to stick up for yourself?" Liang cut in. "Have to get your woman to do your talking. As you don't have the grapefruits."

"Not, not my woman." Mikey bumbled.

"Of course, you fancy her." Rachel retorted. "That's why you're defending her. You've always had a thing for her. Of course, that's your business. But when she starts on like she has today, you need to tell her to button it. She's disrupting the dynamic of our room. Us three in here. We get on well and look out for each other. We don't need her disrupting that."

Mikey was starting to feel the sweat on his back.

"You want to slip little Mikey winkey inside her, don't you?" Liang insinuated. Making a claw movement with his little finger. "It's okay. I can't fault you."

"Liang! Enough!" Rachel blurted out. Offended.

Mikey's heart was palpitating now. He had the urge to throw a volley at Liang. Though, like earlier, the words wouldn't come. He desperately tried. He willed himself to pluck up the courage. None was forthcoming. He slipped out into the kitchen.

The next thing he saw upon returning, was Siobhan walking out of the shop. Glaring at Beth as she went. Sean then emerged and beckoned Beth to follow him back up the stairs.

When they were seated in his office. Sean began. "Beth. I have heard a disturbing report from Siobhan, about an incident that occurred this afternoon. I would like you to tell me about it."

Beth composed herself and started. "It was a simple misunderstanding that got out of hand."

"How so?" Sean asked.

"A customer sent an email to complain that his order was wrong," she stated. As calm as ever. "As it was the first order Liang had done since he joined us. Siobhan assumed that Mikey was to blame, considering he was in charge of his training. I pointed out that I was working on another order with Mikey at the same time. A rather large one. Which is why it took two of us. I remembered Liang making a specific remark regarding an item in the order in question. That is why I knew it was impossible for it to be Mikey, who processed it. I simply pointed this out to Siobhan."

"Ok," Sean said simply. "You are a valued member of my team. But you let your mouth get in the way of your better judgement," he continued, "You have to understand that you were speaking to your manager. The rights and wrongs of what she was doing, are not your concern. You are here to do a job. Not to question the authority of your superiors. There will come a time in your life when you're in a management role. Just like Siobhan is now. You're clearly bright enough for me to have no doubt about that. Then you will realise just how difficult a job it is. For now, you should concentrate on your own role and let Siobhan manage in the way that she sees fit."

"So now you've heard the evidence I've put forward. I take it you will be investigating and when it is found to be correct. You will have Siobhan apologise to Mikey. Not just for being falsely accused. Also, for the way she spoke to him," Beth quietly and sternly worded.

"Have you heard a word I have just said?" Sean asked with

disbelief.

"Yes," Beth replied. "I am just informing you that nobody has the right to speak to anybody the way she did to Mikey this afternoon. I would not let my own mother speak to me in that manner."

"It is not about you, Beth," Sean disbelievingly told her. "I want you to keep your opinions on management matters to yourself. They do not concern you and you have no right to question my processes."

Beth kept her silence. Realising saying any more, would be a pointless exercise.

"Now, enjoy the rest of your afternoon and send Mikey up please," he ordered her. Looking down at the paperwork on his desk.

Beth flipped the middle finger of her left hand, in Sean's direction. After she had closed the door.

Mikey managed to say a quick thank you to Beth, before trundling up to see Sean. She told him. "It's okay. Just watch yourself."

"Mikey. Just a quick word. I know it's home time soon," Sean quietly said as he entered, motioning for him to take a seat. "I know what has transpired in the last few weeks, with regards to the new starters training and so forth."

Mikey didn't know how to respond. So, he just stayed silent.

"It can be difficult for us guys to concentrate on more than one thing at once," Sean continued. "Multi-tasking is what they call it. You see, women are much better at it than us men. We just have to accept that. I want you to work on that and further opportunities will arise in the future. For now, concentrate on your job and your attendance record."

"I feel as if I'm being bullied," Mikey blurted out. Before he had the chance to stop himself.

"What?" asked Sean sharply.

"I, I feel like I'm being bullied," he slowly repeated. "Psychologically bullied."

"By whom?" Sean curiously questioned.

"Rachel and Liang," he answered. He didn't know how or why this notion had just occurred to him. But he felt in his gut, that he was right.

"What? By a woman and a new starter?" Sean mockingly replied. "Give me a break, Mikey."

"Yes," was Mikey's crumbling reply.

"You need to stick up for yourself more," Sean told him. "You have been here for over eighteen months now and I need to see progress with how you communicate with your colleagues. If this doesn't improve and neither does your attendance record, you will be up the road. Am I making myself clear? I have cut you more slack than I should have already. And now you come to me with some half-arsed excuse about a female bullying you. Buck your ideas up. I need to see an improvement to your attitude, and I need to see it fast. Now, have a good evening, Mikey," he spelled out for him.

Mikey's head was all over the place on his way home, from what had transpired that day. He was trying to fathom it out. Did he really think he was being bullied? Or was Sean right? Is he too soft? Of course, he knew he needed to express himself more. But is that weakness? He wasn't sure. He thought. "Over used words are just as dangerous as under used ones." He also knew, he'd had a feeling in his gut about Rachel for a while now. It just hadn't made its home run until now. Liang was a right off. He knew that. But was it really him? Or has Rachel been pulling his strings all along? He needed a way to find out. He needed to think about this. He diverted to Tesco on his way, to pick up four cans of Carlsberg. He needed a drink tonight, but not company. He needed to be alone with his mind. "Just like old times," he thought. Whilst he waited for his beer to chill in the fridge, he wrote,

The mouth that never opens

Jaw locked with words unspoken Wheels not set in motion

The wisdom can be doting

If found, is the healing lotion Express the duress of this mess Success would beckon no less Surprising, is a mind compromising Its feelings to the silence

A veiled state of inside crying A life made of constant lying

Is that mouth that never opens

Chapter 12

Mikey kept to himself the best he could at work the following morning. He was still processing the events of the previous day. Communication was what Sean had said. He knew he needed to figure out an effective way of doing that, if he wanted to keep his job. He didn't feel like he wanted to communicate with Rachel or Liang though.

Yesterday, he had come to the realisation of just how badly they had been treating him. They looked upon him as a lesser being. He knew that now. He needed to show them he was more than that. But how? A theory was starting to take shape in his mind. He thought back to previous times Rachel and himself had proper conversations and what they were about. He understands now that the only times she spoke to him with respect was when it was to her benefit. When the wind suited her sails. If she wanted or needed something from him. When this wasn't the case and it was him that wanted to talk, she was dismissive. She thought the world revolved around her. Every conversation they had, would somehow be brought back to her. Her wants, her needs. If a story was told about something awful. Then you could bet your bottom dollar, something far worse had happened to Rachel. Or somebody she knew. Was Liang also under her spell? Just in a different way. Was she the one telling him to behave the way he was? To give her complete control of their working environment. Or were they in it together? He was hatching a plan and needed to try it out. "Just stay quiet for now," he told himself.

The bad thing had reared its head the previous evening. He had to control it. He had to be better.

Later that evening, a band signed to the Energy label had a gig at the Deaf Institute in Manchester. Mikey knew all employees were expected to attend. Including him. He thought it would be good to have a couple of beers. Then immediately put the brakes on. "Protect yourself," he cautioned. He wasn't ready to let on to his colleagues that he liked a drink now. It was too soon after his absence and it would invoke further suspicion. He didn't want that. Especially after what happened yesterday. Having his usual couple of shandies would be the best course of action. He decided to purchase four beers from Tesco on his way home. That way he could have a drink when he got back, and nobody would be any the wiser. At some point today, he wanted to speak to Liang alone. He had ever really had a chance to have a full one-on-one conversation with him and he needed to test his theory. He just had to bide his time and wait for an opportunity.

As he worked, he listened to the insipid conversation between his two back-office colleagues. It was Rachel bleating on about which were her favourite breeds of dogs and showing pictures as she went. Liang cut in a few times to relay his favourites. To which he was told they were "Typical men's choices."

She did try to involve Mikey in the conversation. He replied. "I'm more of a cat person myself."

To which she turned immediately back to Liang and spoke. "Dogs are much better animals. More loyal."

"There she goes again. Controlling the narrative," he thought. Not letting the discussion deviate from her control.

She went on to say about how her hair felt so smooth and soft today. She had washed it the previous evening, with a new shampoo and conditioner combination she had seen advertised by a model on Twitter. "Nobody cares. You narcissistic fuck," Mikey denounced her in his head.

Sean popped down during lunch time to have a brief, easy going chat with everybody individually. It was nothing formal. And not unusual. Making small talk with his employees, was his way of making them feel like he cared, Mikey knew. When he came to his desk. Sean simply enquired, "Is everything okay?" To which Mikey confirmed it was. Seeing a look in his eyes, that he couldn't quite make out. It was one of concern, mixed with wanting to make sure he was behaving. No doubt hoping that his words from yesterday had sunk in. Siobhan was not to be seen in the office all day. She had gone to prepare everything for the gig tonight. Mikey was sure he would see her there later. "Great," he sarcastically thought.

His opportunity arose in the mid-afternoon to speak to Liang. Another customer that needed dealing with had come into the shop whilst Beth and Tariq were already occupied. As usual, it was Rachel who went to deal with them. This left Mikey a golden opportunity. He couldn't let it slip.

"How are you finding things here?" Mikey innocently asked.

"Not bad," Liang replied. "It can be a little dull with the old timers. But a job's a job, I suppose."

"Yeah," Mikey chirped. Realising staying on his good side would coax the real person. "What have you done before?" he then asked.

"A bit of holiday repping. Worked behind a few bars. That sort of thing," Liang informed him.

"Must be fun. That sort of work?" Mikey queried.

"It has its upsides. Like the talent you get," he reported back.

Mischievously grinning. "The hours are no fun though. They're much better here. Nine to five Monday to Friday. Then 2pm finish on a Saturday."

"Leaves time for fun on a Saturday," Mikey gleamed.

"I'm sure our ideas of fun, are a bit different," Liang flatly replied.

"You might be surprised," Mikey conveyed.

"I doubt that very much," Liang rejected. "You get off on your thing and I get off on mine."

"You should never judge a book by its cover," Mikey told him.

"So, you're telling me you're some sort of secret party animal?" Liang asked with surprise and a piqued level of interest.

"It's always the quiet ones," Mikey smirked back.

"I'm not having that," Liang dismissed.

"We will see tonight, won't we," Mikey announced.

Rachel returned to her back-office workstation, declaring. "I've just spoke to the rudest person."

"Were you speaking to yourself?" Mikey queried in his head.

"What were you two boys conspiring about?" she asked. "I saw you whispering with one another while I was in the shop."

"Nothing for you to worry about." Mikey grinned. Winking to Liang.

"Getting good at this," he thought. He decided that his chat with Liang, had been inconclusive. He needed to see more. He was impressed by the way he controlled the conversation, however. He had been incredibly nervous, though had hidden it much better.

Mikey arrived at the Deaf Institute that evening. Situated on Grosvenor Street, just around the corner from the city's

University. In an Energy Records financed taxi.

Along with Beth and Tariq. Rachel and Liang had got their own taxi, as there were no minibuses available. So, they had to split up in order to accommodate everybody properly. With a normal private hire vehicle only seating a maximum of four passengers. The three of them waited outside for their colleagues to arrive, in order for everybody to enter together.

The first port of call was to the bar. Where Mikey ordered his usual shandy. To which Liang asked, in front of the group. "I thought you were getting on it, tonight?"

"I never said anything about that," Mikey replied. Looking confused.

"You said earlier, about it always being the quiet ones." He insisted.

"Not on a school night. I would never do that. We have work tomorrow," Mikey told him.

Liang looked confused. "Never mind."

Rachel spoke to him. "Let's go and find Siobhan."

"Nicely done," Beth complimented Mikey. After they walked away. With it just being the two of them as Tariq had gone to the toilet.

"I just wanted to make sure nobody thought I was going to get drunk," Mikey shyly responded.

"I know," Beth replied. "I also know that you probably did get drunk, the night before you phoned in sick."

Mikey looked worried.

"It's perfectly okay," she reassured. "The pressure of the situation must have been getting to you and you needed a release. I get it. We all need that sometimes. Just next time, do it when you haven't got work the next day. Hold on until then, won't you?" warmly asking the question.

"I did," he admitted. "I did it. I went out and got drunk. I've never been so drunk in my life. I just didn't wake up when my alarm went off. I was so scared."

Beth turned to check on the whereabouts of Tariq. Noticing he had gone to see Siobhan also. She continued. "It really is all right. I don't feel like coming into work some days when I'm stressed about something. Or would much rather be somewhere else. It's perfectly natural. I just want to fuck everything off sometimes."

Mikey was a bit taken aback by her swearing. As he had never heard her do so before. He spoke, "You always seem to be in control. Always calm and reassuring. Like, with what happened with Siobhan yesterday. She was losing it all over the place with you and, you just kept so calm and composed. Put her right back in her place."

"It was the swan you see on the water," she replied. "Calm on the surface and frantically moving its legs under water. Out of sight. I was bricking myself the whole time. I have learnt to hide that from the people I don't want to see it. My boyfriend, Rob, bears the brunt of it when I'm home. Bless him."

"I, I just wanted to say thank you," Mikey fumbled somewhat, "for yesterday with Siobhan. I appreciate what you did for me. It mustn't have been easy and could easily have got you into trouble as well." He spoke more calmly as he went on.

"You should never get into trouble for telling the truth," Beth told him. "I simply outlined the mistake that had been made and if Siobhan's ego is so out of control, that she doesn't want to listen. Then that is her issue, not ours. Same goes for Sean. He had the same attitude when I spoke to him as well. Banging on about how I shouldn't question authority. I believe authority is there to be questioned, in a civilised society. If the person in charge is fair and just. They should have no reason not to answer questions about their decisions. If not for nothing but to alleviate any fears those under their influence may have. Remain open minded when asked and if they find they have made a mistake. Be humble enough to accept it and apologise. Only weak, power-hungry leaders can't do that. Sean and Siobhan have shown me that they are driven by power and control. Which is sad. Most people are that way, I have found. Not you though. You're different. I can sense it. That doesn't make you worse than anybody else. In fact, it makes you better than most people."

"Thank you, Beth. That means a lot," Mikey replied, with emotion in his voice. "You are too. You are so kind and generous. Always so willing to help others and don't power trip. You could easily do so. You're clearly more intelligent than all of us."

"Where would that get me?" she asked. "It would make me just like them. If it wasn't for my uni fees and having to pay rent on my apartment. I would probably have quit yesterday. After the way I was spoken to. But it's not so easy to do that when you have responsibilities," she admitted.

"Why did you not go into further education when you left school?" Mikey asked.

"I had a dead-beat father who left my mum to raise four children on her own," Beth confided. "We had very little money. My mum worked three jobs to provide for us.

"With me being the oldest, I decided to get a job when I left school. To help her out. Now with my siblings grown up, I have managed to get myself on my evening course."

"That's such a selfless thing to do," he gushed to her. "I don't see many others doing that."

"Most wouldn't," she agreed. "What did Sean say to you when you went to see him?"

"Lectured me," he spoke. "I told him something that I never even knew was in my head until the words came out," Mikey confided.

"What was it?" Beth asked.

"I told him I was being bullied by Rachel and Liang," Mikey answered. Not meeting her gaze.

"How did he respond?" she probed.

"Couldn't understand how I could possibly be bullied, by a female and a new starter," Mikey disclosed.

"He clearly doesn't understand there are different types of bullying, does he?" Beth shot back with a venom Mikey hadn't heard before. "I'm sorry for raising my voice."

She immediately apologised. "It's just that has made me angry. You confided in him something very serious, and he mocked you. I think even less of him now than I did after yesterday's performance with me. He should never have said that to you. He has no right to do so. He has a duty of care to you, as an employee and he has failed."

"He told me to buck my ideas up with my communication with others. Or I would be out the door," Mikey went on.

"It's not you who needs to buck their ideas up," she refuted. "I wouldn't want to lose you as a colleague and a friend. But would it be possible for you to just leave? It might be better in the long run," she asked. Worrying that he may take it the wrong way and think she wanted rid of him as well.

"I can't. I'm the same as you," he answered. "I have responsibilities too. Like keeping my flat." Sensing what she was thinking. He alleviated her worries. "I know you didn't just say what you did, because you don't want to be associated with me. I understand you said it with my best interests at heart."

"I did. And I'm thankful that you understand," she expressed. "You are a wonderful guy. Who deserves to be treated so much better than you have been. You're fantastic to be around. I adore the fact that we're colleagues and friends. You're awesome at both. You will make a wonderful husband for a lucky lady one day as well. Jeez, if I didn't have a boyfriend, you would be under consideration." She playfully informed him. Smiling.

"Maybe…" Mikey began.

"I have a boyfriend. who I'm very happy with, Mikey," she cut him off. "You will meet somebody. Now, let's go and enjoy the show," she encouraged. Linking his arm to walk. "Just make sure you stay on the shandies tonight." Beth cautioned. A few moments later.

The Protons played a decent set that night and it was enjoyed by all. After the show, the drinks started to flow. However, Mikey made good on his promise to Beth about the shandy. He was surprised to find himself thinking about getting some more of the goodies that he and Colin had enjoyed. It was pointless to even think about it. As he had nobody to get any off and the last thing he wanted was for Colin to show up.

Coming out of the toilets, he noticed Tariq getting more than friendly with a lady. Tariq noticed him watching and gave him an alarmed look. Mikey just smiled at him and thought, "None of my business."

What was more of interest, was the way he saw Rachel and Liang fondling each other. With Liang doing most of the action. He thought. "They're both as bad as each other. She's getting what she wants. And it looks like, he's getting what he wants tonight."

He left in a taxi with Beth a little later and left the others to it.

When he returned home and drank a couple of his Carlsberg stash, he thought about everything and started to speak to himself, out loud. "I Don't want to be near any of them. None of them. Except Beth and Tom. They're the only good ones, as far as I can see. I don't want to be anywhere near the human race. Their egos are out of control. All I meet are egocentric, narcissistic boneheads. They are ill. Every single one of them.

They race to see who can outshine the other. Who can have a bigger this, a better that. When all the while, missing the point. You should concentrate on making yourself and everybody around you, better. You are ill! I want a better car than him. You are ill! I want a bigger house to make me feel good. You are ill! You are FUCKING ILL! Just be better than you were yesterday."

"The hardest thing to do is to forgive yourself. Human compassion? The sad thing is, nobody wants to know you when you don't fit in. You know why? Very few people have the intellect to understand that your behaviour, is due to your mental defects. Most of the ones that can, don't give a shit. A sad tale of the gluttonous, self-serving, stink hole that is humanity. YOU ARE ILL! NOT ME!"

"Beth has taught me that one person, with courage can make a majority. I was a stupid, stupid man to fall for their tricks and let them take advantage of my naivety. You may say that they're solely to blame, but no! Everybody has a role to play, and you must take responsibility for your own actions. Otherwise, there is no learning or growth. I've been trying to go home my whole life. Everybody is trying to make it home. Wherever that may be. Or whatever that may mean. Stupid people who think they're intelligent. Are the most dangerous people in the world. I've realised the bullshit said about me, is for the purpose of that person's own ego and status. It makes me incredibly sad, that I don't believe anybody in this world knows the real me. I've realised speaking the truth only upsets people, as it offends their egos. As they hide behind a veil of illusion and insecurity. Am I thinking clearly now? I guess some flowers, take longer to bloom than others."

Chapter 13

"Can you meet me in Wilkinson's car park before work, please?" was the text message from Tariq that Mikey woke up to the following morning.

"Yeah, sure," was Mikey's two-word reply. Feeling somewhat groggy from the previous evening. He instantly knew what it would be about. He asked himself. "What was I ranting about last night?" It was people. He knew he had gone in, hard. Perhaps went a bit too far. He was gloriously thankful that nobody else was around to hear him. They would have thought he was a madman. After he made his bed, he got the clothes he wanted to wear out of the wardrobe, set them down on the made bed. "Another step," he said aloud.

He made his way to the car park to meet Tariq. With Wilkinson's being a two second walk past Energy Records, it was not a stretch. Though he did need to walk past the shop in order to reach it. He knew there would be no issue with this, as he and Tariq generally opened up anyway. So, nobody should be there to notice. They weren't and he safely made it to the car park behind Wilkinson's. Walking through the walkway that separated the two shops. There he saw Tariq, already waiting.

"Mikey," He greeted him. "How's your head?"

"Not too bad," Mikey responded. "Stayed on the shandy last night."

"Mine's pounding." Tariq grimaced. "Good night though, yeah." He beamed.

"Yeah, I enjoyed it." Mikey agreed. Somewhat flatly. Eager for the conversation to move onto its real subject.

"I just want to talk about what you saw me doing," Tariq nervously spoke.

"It's none of my business," Mikey quickly jumped in.

"I just wanted to make sure, you're not going to say anything," Tariq pleaded.

"What you do is your business, not mine," Mikey told him. "You don't need to worry about me saying anything. I can assure you that your secret's safe with me."

"Cheers, mate. I appreciate it," Tariq thanked him.

"No worries," Mikey responded. "As long as you had a good time," he grinned.

"I sure did," Tariq beamed and they both laughed. "Now, let's get the shop opened. Before anybody notices us skulking around in car parks."

With that they made the short walk and opened up to go about their usual morning routines.

When Liang entered. Tariq instantly walked up to him and spoke. "A word in the kitchen."

They both walked into the empty room and Liang quizzically asked. "What's up, man?"

"I want you to back off Mikey," he flatly told him.

"What do you mean?" Liang innocently asked.

"The way you speak to him," Tariq told him. "Always trying to put him down. He's my mate and I won't stand for it. The way you have acted with him, makes you a bully.

And I don't do bullies. It makes him upset. I'm not the type of guy who likes to see my mates upset. Now, what do you have to say about that?" he laid out to him. With a look in his eye, that meant business.

"I never meant any offence," Liang tried to pacify.

"You knew what you were doing," Tariq contested. "Have the balls to admit it."

"If I've been out of order, I'm sorry. I apologise," Liang pleaded.

"Typical bully, aren't you?" Tariq insinuated. "Give it the big 'uns and then crumble when confronted. Let me tell you something, Mikey's a good lad. If I ever see you so much as utter one word to him that is out of order you will have me to deal with.

And next time, it won't just be talking. Now, get the fuck out of my sight."

Liang sloped off to his desk, without another word. Where Mikey was already seated. He didn't dare say anything to him. Not after what Tariq had just done. So, just reciprocated Mikey's good morning and fired up his laptop.

"Oh, what a night!" Rachel entered, clutching a bottle of water and a McDonalds double sausage and egg McMuffin. "Needed," she added upon taking her first bite. "Glad to see you behaved yourself last night," she addressed Mikey.

"Unlike some," he said in his head. Though spoke. "School night, Rachel. I'm not the one clutching heart disease in a sandwich."

"You're cheeky today," she fumed. "Plus, anyway, Maccie Ds isn't as calorific as it used to be. Not that it's any of your business."

"Liang," she purred attempting to change the subject.

Mikey did not let her. "Still tasty though, right?" he mischievously asked.

"Yes," was her absent reply, trying to engage Liang.

"I've always preferred a full English in the morning myself,"

Mikey informed her.

"Nice," she threw back looking agitated.

"What's the go to takeaway choice after a night out?" Mikey probed. "I don't really do nights out. But I do love a good Indian."

"What's with all the questions?" Rachel retaliated.

"Just making conversation," he harmlessly replied.

"Well, don't," she fired back, losing her cool a bit more.

"Why not?" he asked. Looking confused. "Just a bit of team bonding, is all."

"Listen, Mikey," she chastised him, "I've got a hangover and I haven't got the time for your nonsense. Concentrate on your work."

"Cut him some slack," Liang interposed.

"You sticking up for him now?" she vehemently asked.

"Is this trouble in paradise?" was the sarcastic question Mikey asked himself.

"No. Just, all he's doing is trying to talk to you," Liang quietly told her.

"I feel trouble brewing at the mill," Mikey laughed to himself.

"Well, he should know that I haven't got time now. I've told him already." Rachel bolted. Her eyes burning now.

"He's just being friendly. We're a team here. Come on, Rach," Liang pleaded.

"Sticking together with your guy mates. Is that how it is?" she accused.

"Not at all," he tried to placate. "We all had a great night last night and you're feeling a little hungover. I'm just saying, there's no need to take that out on Mikey. That's all."

"You fucking men are all the same!" she declared. Raising

her voice and stomping off into the kitchen.

"Aww. Was your Liang winky not good enough to satisfy. What a shame," Mikey chuckled to himself.

The rest of the morning passed with Rachel and Liang doing their level best to ignore each other. Mikey thought about stirring the pot a bit more. But he decided he had done enough damage for one day. He thought it best to leave the rats in their nests.

Just before lunch time, Rachel broke the silence excitedly. "I'm getting a new apartment! Daddy has just confirmed that he will pay the deposit and first month's rent for me. I've been buttering him up for ages."

"That's nice," Mikey spoke back. Looking up only briefly. Not really wanting to engage in a full-blown conversation.

"I'm Daddy's little princess and I always get what I want," she declared. "Are you not excited for me, Liang?"

"Yeah, of course," he calmly spoke to her. Waking from his slumber. "Whereabouts, is it?"

"Want to know where it is? Is that so you can come around unexpectedly and take advantage of me?" she teased.

"Wouldn't dream of it," Liang grinned.

"What a little liar you are," she playfully ribbed him.

"Complete gentleman, me," Liang rebuffed. Holding his arms up and showing his open palms to her.

"Jeez. I need to get out of here," Mikey said to himself. "Leave the little love birds to it."

"Does anybody want anything from Tesco?" he asked out loud.

"I'm okay, thanks," Liang politely replied.

"How can I think about that now?" Rachel posed. "I need to think what décor I'm having. Furniture. What style I want my bathroom and bedroom. What pieces of art I can get off Daddy.

So many things to decide. I'm excited!" She went on. More to herself with each passing word.

Mikey slipped out unnoticed. Enquired as to whether Beth or Tariq required anything. Which they didn't. And headed towards his destination.

He met Mr Jefferson in the pub after work that day. It was a planned meeting this time. Mr Jefferson had come into the shop during the afternoon and managed to get Mikey on his own. Asking him if he, "Fancied a pint later?" To which Mikey replied in the affirmative.

Knowing what time Mikey would finish work. Mr Jefferson was already seated at their usual table when Mikey arrived. With a pint of Carlsberg ready for him.

"Evening, Mikey?" was how he greeted him.

"Good evening," Mikey replied. "Thanks for the drink."

"No worries. Thought I would have one ready for you," Mr Jefferson declared. He leaned forward and whispered. "Your girlfriend's working today."

Mikey was flummoxed. "I don't have one."

"I mean Tanya." He winked.

"It's not her shift today," Mikey mumbled. Feeling a bit hot under the collar.

"Perhaps she's covering somebody else's," Mr Jefferson suggested. "You'll see. She will be back in a minute. Only gone to change a barrel in the cellar. I told her you were coming in and she was delighted." His eyes sparkled to his companion.

"I, I don't know what to do," Mikey stammered.

"Just play it cool," Mr Jefferson told him. "Ask her how she is. Make a bit of small talk. Let her know you're interested in getting to know her."

"What small talk?" Mikey asked.

"Anything you like," Mr Jefferson answered. "Just don't mention the weather. If I had a pound for every time I heard. 'Weathers nice, isn't it?' or. 'Cold today, isn't it?' By some guy. I would be a millionaire," he declared.

Tanya smiled in Mikey's direction upon re-entering the bar area and he shyly reciprocated.

Mr Jefferson chuckled and asked. "How was work?"

"Better after what happened the other day," Mikey told him.

"What happened?"

Mr Jefferson listened in silence, as Mikey relayed the incident with Siobhan and how Beth had leapt to his defence. He gave an account more vivid and detailed than he thought he would. Upon getting to the part about him telling Sean that he thought he was being bullied. Mr Jefferson interrupted. "What did Seany boy say?"

"Told me I need to stick up for myself more and thought it ridiculous. The fact that I said it was a female and a new starter." Mikey confessed. "Told me I need to buck my ideas up."

"The poncy little prick!" Mr Jefferson quietly, though furiously asserted. "Wait until I have a word with him. Thinking he can get away with speaking to you like that.

Watch what happens if he tries it with me."

"Please don't do that," Mikey pleaded.

"Why not?" Mr Jefferson fired back.

"Because I'm dealing with it," Mikey told him.

"How so?" Mr Jefferson asked. Calmer now.

"I'm learning to control conversations more," Mikey confided. "The last couple of days. I have had conversations with both Rachel and Liang. That I have been in complete control of. I see them for what they are now. They're manipulative and want to be in control of everything. I'm not going to let them be. I'm going to control the narrative from now on."

"That's good." Mr Jefferson confirmed. "So, you understand now that they are not your friends. They do not want the best for you. They only want the best for themselves. Sadly, most people are this way."

"I see it perfectly now," Mikey agreed.

"You need to tread carefully, though," Mr Jefferson informed him.

"How so?"

"Office politics are a lot like the butterfly effect. Every action has a reaction. So, you have to work out what the consequences might be before you act," Mr Jefferson intently spelled out to him.

"Weigh up the pros and cons. Then their possible next moves?" Mikey asked. Grasping it.

"Exactly. You're a bright boy," Mr Jefferson complimented. "One thing you have to do though, is make sure you look after Beth. She is quite the young lady, that one. Very genuine. Which can't be said of a lot of people. Do your best to protect her from all of this."

"I will. I promise. She deserves it," Mikey reassured.

"I should have said something to Liang, though." He remembered, "He mocked me when Tariq was encouraging me to take up boxing. Tariq said I might enjoy it and to give it a go."

"Not all men have to be fighters," Mr Jefferson told him. "What is it that you're actually interested in? Concentrate on that."

"Poetry," was his simple reply.

"Interesting," Mr Jefferson pondered. "Are you any good?"

"I don't know. I've never let anybody read any of it before,"

Mikey confided.

"Well, let me have a look sometime," Mr Jefferson encouraged. "I love good lyrics in the music I listen to. So, I would be honoured to give your poems a read."

"Thank you," Mikey exuded. "They're all in my flat."

"Well, one evening. Why don't I come round to your flat? We can grab a few beers and some fish 'n' chips along the way. Then read those lyrical joys of yours," Mr Jefferson smiled at him.

"Sounds good to me," Mikey confirmed. "Do you want another drink?" he asked

"One for the road. Why not?"

"Hello again," Tanya greeted him.

"Hi," Mikey replied

"Here again. Are we?" she teased.

"Just, just a quick few," he stumbled.

"I'm just kidding," Tanya reassured. "It's nice to see you again."

"It's nice to see you too." Mikey smiled.

"You have a nice smile. You should use it more often," Tanya complimented.

"Your eyes are beautiful," Mikey spilled out. Aghast that he didn't manage to stop himself.

"Thank you. That's sweet of you to say," Tanya flirted. "Unfortunately, these eyes of mine will only be seeing this bar tonight. I'm covering until closing."

"Oh. That's a shame," Mikey lamented.

"Although, I do finish at five on Saturday," she informed him, playing with her hair.

"If you're not busy. Erm… I can have a drink here after you finish." Mikey was doing all he could to stop from trembling by this point.

"You mean us, together?" "Well, erm…"

"I would love to," Tanya confirmed. "Don't come in too early though. I don't want you drunk before I finish," she laughed.

"I will come in about half four. If okay?" he nervously asked.

"Perfect for me. See you then."

"See you then," Mikey repeated.

"Now, you best get back to your old man over there. He's probably getting lonely," Tanya joked and they both laughed.

"Chalk one up for the underdogs," Mikey smirked to his companion.

"Do tell," Mr Jefferson encouraged.

"I'm meeting Tanya for drinks after her shift on Saturday." Mikey beamed. Completely unable to keep the smile off his face.

"I knew you could do it," Mr Jefferson encouraged, ruffling his hair. "You little rascal." They both laughed.

Tanya kept her gaze on this exchange and warmly smiled to herself upon viewing it.

Chapter 14

"Why did I ask her for a drink?" Mikey screamed to himself. As he made the short walk from his apartment, to meet Tanya in the White Lion. He was fumbling all over himself. Constantly scratching his head and doing his upmost to stop his body from convulsing. He decided not to cross the road that led to the pub. He instead turned right, past the HSBC bank and decided he needed a walk around the block. He needed to steel himself. He continued walking past Yates and did not turn into Broad Street. His head was swimming now. He instead, continued walking and crossed over at the Knowsley. He walked through the bus station over the road and continued until he reached the market. There he stopped and said to himself. "I can't do this. Just continue walking and you never have to go in there again. You never have to see Tanya again. You can just leave it all behind. This could never have been a good idea. What was I thinking?"

He sat upon one of the benches outside the entrance for the market for a couple of minutes. Feeling angry with himself now for even thinking about backing out. He had to go. He wanted to go. "Find the courage," he spelled out to himself. His hands visibly shaking that much, he put them in his pockets. Hoping nobody was watching. "I just don't know what to do," was the desperate thought running through his head. Eventually, he rose. Took a deep breath and said to himself. "You have to do this. You have to do this. Keep the bad thing out of your mind and do this."

He walked through the revolving door of the pub at five to

five. Just about making it before Tanya's shift finished. Upon seeing him she greeted him., "I didn't think you were coming."

"Was just getting ready, is all," Mikey lied.

"Well, you look nice," Tanya complimented.

"Thank you. And so do you," Mikey reciprocated.

"Carlsberg?" she asked.

"Yes please," he responded. Then thought, "Tom said get her a drink too." So, he stumbled somewhat, "An, and whatever you would like."

"Why, thank you." Tanya beamed. "I will have a Bailey's, please."

Tanya poured the drinks and Mikey went to sit at the usual table he sat at with Mr Jefferson. Sue was already there to spell Tanya and knowing what was transpiring, she took over the bar a couple of minutes early. They sat for a few moments in silence. Mikey feverishly trying to think of something to say to break the ice when Tanya smiled and asked, "How are you?"

"I, I'm good. How are you?" Mikey politely responded. Doing his utmost to keep his voice level.

"I'm very well, thank you. I'm glad you came," Tanya responded.

"I thought you might change your mind," Mikey timidly said. Not meeting her gaze.

"Why would I do that?" Tanya innocently asked.

"Just, just thought you would," Mikey fumbled.

"And miss out on a free Bailey's?" she joked raising her glass. Her sultry dark eyes melting into Mikey's as he was now eventually looking at her.

"Least I could do," he smiled back. "I like your hair," he complimented, noticing she had red highlights in her long dark hair.

"Thank you," Tanya gushed. "I got it done yesterday. I'm always playing about with it. Trying out new styles and hoping to get one that suits."

"This one suits you just fine," Mikey flattered.

"Aren't you the charmer," she teased, stroking her freshly highlighted hair.

"How was your shift?" Mikey anxiously asked. Feeling a little nervous with her flirty behaviour.

"It was a bit dull. Very quiet," Tanya lamented. "Mr Jefferson came in earlier. Had a couple of pints and left about four."

"To get his fish 'n' chips," Mikey suddenly jumped in. Feeling a sudden sense of guilt for interrupting.

Tanya didn't seem to mind and responded. "Yeah, every Saturday the same. Who is he to you anyway? A relative? Uncle or something?"

"No. He just comes into my work quite often," Mikey informed her. His heart rate slowing further by now. "He's our best customer. Always in there buying something. At least once a week."

"Where do you work?" Tanya asked.

"Energy Records on The Rock," Mikey answered.

"Nice," Tanya smiled. "Do you enjoy it?"

"Yeah," Mikey responded. Quickly realising he needed to say a bit more. Not too much though. Probably best not to go into all the problems he'd been experiencing. "I love music. So, it's a good fit," he managed.

"Classical music for me," Tanya told him. "Most people think that's a bit sad."

"I don't. Most people don't understand things properly," Mikey reassured her. "I mainly like guitar music. But do admire classical music as well."

"You're different to most, aren't you?" Tanya perceived.

"Erm, yeah, I don't know what to make of it though." Mikey was feeling a little more nervous now. What if she thought he was strange?

"It's a good thing," Tanya assured. "I would take individuality over somebody pretending just to fit in. Any day of the week. Just be yourself, is what I say. Then the right people will naturally gravitate towards you. If you pretend to be somebody you're not. You will end up getting involved with the wrong people."

"I've always thought I never belonged," Mikey conceded.

"I have had those thoughts too," Tanya admitted. "I used to really struggle with it. Then I realised that I just needed to let go of the social stigmas. Nobody is perfect and the more we try to be the further away from our true selves we get."

"Just be yourself?" Mikey asked.

"Exactly," she confirmed. "If you do that. What wasn't meant to be, will drift away and you'll be left with what was meant. If you go the other way though, you'll end up with what wasn't."

"I've started to grow by getting a good routine for my day," Mikey told her.

"That's good," Tanya noted. "I could do with an orderly routine to my day. I'm a bit hectic," she admitted.

"Do you make your bed in the morning?" Mikey suddenly asked.

"Wouldn't you like to know? You cheeky boy." Tanya laughed.

Mikey blushed. "I only asked as it's what I started with."

"I'm just teasing you." Tanya tilted her head to inform him.

"I want to hear what you mean?"

"It's about getting a routine," he told her. "Start by making your bed when you get out of it in the morning. Then add something new each day. Before you know it, you will have an orderly routine. That you can feel good about. It will naturally make you feel better about yourself."

"Aren't you the clever one," Tanya complimented. "It's a bit like the world we live in. If the human race did one thing better each day. Before we knew it, we would be living in a society we could be proud of."

"Exactly the same concept," Mikey agreed. "What do you think we could do better?" he asked.

"We should start by treating each other better," she started. "Stop all the nonsensical killing and barbaric behaviour. Fighting over trivial things and sending people off to die in wars that only benefit the elite."

"I agree with that," Mikey confirmed. "Most wars are started for political reasons and for one side's gain, in that respect."

"Exactly," Tanya purred. "Then we can move onto stopping killing animals for food. There really is no need for that. I have been a vegetarian since I was a teenager. I don't miss meat one bit. We have meat substitutes now that are just as good for you and the rest, we can get off the land ourselves."

"You mean grow our own food?" he quizzed.

"Yes," she confirmed. "Stop relying on massive supermarket chains and take back control. Live in a society where we look after our own produce and source it locally. Where everybody chips in to make the community as a whole, better."

"I somewhat agree with that," Mikey pondered. "I do like meat, though. I see it as survival of the fittest in the wild. If a cow needed to eat us to survive, it would. I don't see it as anything different."

"You have to see we don't need to do that anymore," Tanya hit back. "Back when we didn't have the resources to make substitutes for those nutrients we need, then yes. But now, we can make whatever we like and live a healthy life."

"But I don't agree with you," Mikey responded. A little louder than he wanted to. Then quietened with, "I'm not going to go live in a log cabin and eat mushrooms. I'm not."

Tanya laughed. "I like this side of you Mikey. Standing up for what you believe in."

"I didn't mean to offend," he offered.

"It's quite all right. We don't have to agree on everything," she informed him. "Now, how about another drink?"

"I will get them."

"Okay."

Mikey returned with the drinks and Tanya spoke. "Don't make it obvious. But see that guy over there?" Quickly diverting her eyes to a slender man in his late twenties. With gelled black hair, sitting on the other side of the pub.

Mikey gave him a covert glance and responded, "Yes."

"Makes my skin crawl." Tanya shuddered.

"Why?"

"He has a problem with the word, consent," she condemned.

"Has he hurt you?" Mikey asked. Getting defensive about her.

"No, not me," Tanya calmed him. Patting him on the arm.

"It was a girl he met on a night out," she told him. "She was very drunk, and he ended up taking her back to his place. Started getting frisky with her. When she came to her senses, told him to stop. He didn't listen and carried on."

"Did she go to the police?" Mikey questioned.

"Yes," Tanya replied hotly, "they told her that enough consent was given. Because she agreed to go back to his. Said the fact that she did this and the way she was dressed. Made it look like she was asking for it. It's disgusting."

"I agree," Mikey confirmed, calmly. "A lady has the right to dress any way she likes. It doesn't give anybody the right to touch her. If she just wants a good night out and says no. Then that should be the end of it."

"You're a sweet guy," Tanya fluttered her eyelashes at him. "You're definitely one of the good ones."

"It's, it's just right," Mikey uneasily stammered.

"I know. But not everybody sees it that way," she judged. Then went on, "I mean, do guys not hear us when we say 'No?' Perhaps we should just steal your stuff and say. 'I'm sorry officer, but he was clearly asking for it. All dressed up with his Rolex watch on. I mean, he was just begging me to steal it. With it being out in the open and all.' He said 'No! I can't have it.' But as has already been publicly stated, the word no has many different meanings. So, I was confused. I thought he was begging me to take it. Why else would he flash it in front of my face?"

"I couldn't agree more with that analogy," Mikey complimented.

"I'm lucky to be with a gentleman tonight." Tanya smiled.

"I'm the lucky one," Mikey told her.

The conversation continued over a couple more drinks. With Tanya telling Mikey about her family background the fact that she has one brother and they both still live with their parents, in the Walmersley area of the town about five minutes' walk from the town centre. Mikey told her about him having being adopted and not knowing about his biological parents. He did leave out the details about his adopted father and there was no way, he was going to tell her about the bad thing.

"Another one?" Mikey asked after the fourth drink.

"I think it's about time you showed me this apartment of yours," Tanya suggested.

"Ok," was all Mikey could manage.

"Lead the way," Tanya told him.

Mikey led her up the stairs to his apartment. Silently praying that Colin wouldn't appear. He didn't and he had much relief when he closed the door.

"What would you like me to do?" Tanya suggestively asked. When the door was closed. Swaying her hips to one side.

Mikey felt a sudden urge he had not felt in a long time and before he could stop himself. Instructed her. "I want you to steal me, like you would a Rolex."

Wordlessly they entered the bedroom. Taking each other's clothes off as they went. Until reaching the bed. After a good round of foreplay, Tanya lay waiting for Mikey to enter her. Which he did. Nervously at first. Getting better with each thrust, as she kissed and caressed him. Feeling her warm breath and eyes melting into his. Mikey thought. "This must be what heaven feels like."

Chapter 15

Mikey woke the next morning, with a feeling of calm all around him. Tanya lay sleeping next to him. It was a strange and new feeling for him. With being so used to waking alone and anxious about what the day may bring. He knew he liked this much better. He wanted to stay in this moment forever. He didn't want to go and see the outside world ever again. He wanted to stay with Tanya. Of course, he knew that he must. For now, he wanted to savour every last second of this. Nothing else mattered to him. He wanted to spend the day lazing in bed with the beautiful young lady beside him. He felt extremely lucky to have her with him. A smile came across his face when he realised, just how much progress he had made. Could he make this work? Could he possibly form a long-lasting relationship with Tanya? The bad thing would surely become a thing of the past, if he could. The future would be bright and blissful. They could eventually get a place of their own and get married. In time, children together. Tom had told him to seize this opportunity if it ever came along.

He was going to make sure he did. He was going to be perfect. Treat Tanya like the queen that she is. Make her happy and give her no reason to ever want to leave him. He decided he should first make his sleeping beauty a nice breakfast and bring it to her in bed. Carefully, he slid the covers aside, as not to wake her and slipped out into the kitchen.

He looked in his fridge and cupboards to see what supplies he had in. Delighted to find he had most of the ingredients to make a full English breakfast. Just as he was taking the bacon out of the fridge, he remembered. "No. She's a vegetarian." What an absolute mess that would have been. He laughed to himself as he put everything back. "What to make instead?" He said out loud. He decided to keep it simple and just make coffee and toast. Which he did so and took it back into the bedroom.

Where he found Tanya had woken up. "Good morning," she greeted him.

"Good morning," he warmly responded. "Thought you might like some breakfast."

"Breakfast in bed." Tanya laughed. "What a thoughtful guy you are."

"I didn't know what you liked," Mikey said hesitantly. "So, I just made some toast."

"Toast is perfect. Thank you," she soothed him.

"Enjoy," Mikey encouraged, taking back his place under the covers.

"Last night was fun," Tanya spoke. With her eyes seducing him all over again.

"It was special," Mikey grinned.

Tanya laughed and teased, "Why you're full of compliments. You weren't bad yourself."

"I hope I made you happy?" Mikey asked. With a hint of pleading to his voice.

"Of course, you did," Tanya assured him. "There's no need to be insecure about it. You did your job well."

"Job?" Mikey questioned.

"A figure of speech," Tanya told him. "Lighten up. We had a wonderful night."

"I'm sorry," he conceded. "I'm just trying to make everything perfect."

"And I'm grateful for that," she comforted him. "You just don't have to try so hard. You're naturally good company. So, just go with the flow."

"Okay," Mikey agreed. "How do you like your toast?" he asked.

"It's certainly set me up for the day," Tanya told him. "It's sweet that you remembered I'm a vegetarian and didn't bring me bacon butties," she laughed.

"The thought never crossed my mind. I remembered what you told me last night," Mikey lied. Thinking it best not to tell her how close she came to receiving a full English. He did think that was a downside. With her being a vegetarian. Would he be able to enjoy a full English breakfast ever again? Would it offend her if he made one for himself? He decided it would be best not to bring this up just yet. Instead, he asked. "What do you want to do today?"

"I'm working a four to closing shift." She informed him. "Remember, I told you that I work on Sunday evenings?"

"Oh yes, of course," Mikey suddenly remembered. "Maybe we could hang out and watch some TV before you have to go to work?"

"I need to get myself home first," Tanya articulated. "Not that I don't want to spend time with you. It's just I need a change of clothes. It wouldn't look too good if I turned up for work, wearing the same clothes as yesterday."

"I suppose not," Mikey had to concede. He hadn't thought of that.

Sensing his uneasiness and feelings of rejection. Tanya pleasantly spoke. "We can do this again sometime. It would make me happy if we could do so. I enjoy spending time with you. But we need to take this slowly. I'm not ready for a full-blown relationship yet. I have recently split from an arsehole ex and I'm not looking for commitment at the moment. You're a sweet guy. I just want us to have some fun, enjoy each other's company and see where it takes us. It's too soon for us to be getting attached."

Feeling a little crestfallen. Mikey replied, "Ok. I just enjoy being with you and want to spend time with you."

"And I do with you," she reassured him. "Look, we're both young and have years in front of us to think about the future. For now, let's enjoy ourselves, have fun and enjoy each other's company. If we're right for each other, I'm sure we will eventually get the three-bed semi and a couple of kids. Just don't think too deeply about it right now, is all."

"I feel I would like that with you," Mikey confided. "But for now. You're right. Let's enjoy ourselves whilst we're still young enough to do so."

"That's better." Tanya smiled. "Now. I need to shower. Let's be thankful that we have each other to have fun with. I like you, Mikey. But let's cool down and simmer. Let's not rush things."

"Ok," Mikey agreed. "I'm afraid I only have Lynx shower gel," he playfully told her.

"That's okay. I will make do," she warmly replied. "You just remember to make the bed."

"Is that the sound of the balloon popping again?" Mikey thought to himself. As she left the room.

Once Tanya had left, Mikey didn't know what to make of it. Had she just blown him out? Or was it him wanting too much too soon? His head was exploding with thoughts of rejection. He just wanted her to be with him. He desperately wanted to move things forward with her. Wanted her to fall in love with him. He asked himself whether that was even possible for a guy like him. Surely, she would get bored of him at some point. See that he has very little experience with this type of thing and move on from him. Decide that he is not good enough for her and find somebody who is. He had to do everything in his power to not let this happen. Had to make it work with her. He would surely not get an opportunity with anybody else, so this was his only chance. He told himself that he had come too far, to go back to sitting in his living room praying for company. He knew now that he had a bit of courage. After all, it took courage to walk into the White Lion alone. Like he had the first time he had a drink with Tom. To ask Tanya out for a drink was a brave thing to do. So was actually going through with it. He had done it. Now was the time for the next step. Which was to make a good life with her. There was nothing more he wanted in that moment. But how to make it possible? She had told him, they needed to take things slowly and build a relationship. Is that normal? Or is it because she's not really that interested? Just waiting until something better comes along. He decided to respect her wishes and not push things. Give her some space and see where it leads. He concluded that it was perfectly acceptable to make himself that full English after all. Then he was going for a beer. Not in the White Lion though. Where Tanya would be. He perilously thought that Colin would be a good solution today.

He knocked on Colin's door about an hour later. He answered and enthused. "Mikey! You coming to the pub for the game?"

"What game?" Mikey asked. A bit taken aback.

"United and Liverpool today, mate," Colin informed him. Like it was something everybody should be aware of.

"I just wanted to see if you fancied a beer?" Mikey numbly asked.

"Yeah, going to head to the Knowsley soon. You coming?" Colin responded.

"Yeah, I could do with a beer," Mikey told him.

"Good lad!" Colin encouraged. "I will get on the blower and get us some stuff. You can put your hand in your pocket and chip fifty to this time."

"I, I don't have cash on me," Mikey stammered.

"I will get it," Colin calmed him. "You just stop off at the cash machine on the way and pay me back."

"Ok," Mikey mumbled back. Unsure as to how or why he had just agreed to it.

"Nice one!" Colin delightedly spoke. "Knock on for you in about half an hour."

"No worries," Mikey answered.

Mikey went back into his apartment, with a sense of dizziness about him. He had been the one who wanted to invite Colin out for a beer. Though it turned out the other way round. How had that happened? He had no interest in who was playing football. He hated the game. He couldn't see the fascination with a bunch of grown men kicking a ball around a field. He couldn't comprehend how much animosity it caused between rival supporters either. How they would fight with each other if one or the other lost. Where was the sense in that? It was just a game, and they took it far too seriously. He used to hate PE at school. He dreaded having to play most of the various different sports he was forced to partake in. He did enjoy rounders and was actually pretty good at it. The other boys would mock him for it and say it was a girls' sport. Tell him that he was a pouf for liking it. He knew now that this was a complete lack of understanding on their part. Everybody was entitled to like anything that they chose and there was nothing wrong with that. Everybody is free to make their own choices. He did wonder whether those boys, who would by now be men would have the same views now? Or was it just their childish behaviour? As they had not fully matured by then.

Colin knocked on around forty minutes later and instantly asked. "Quick one before we head out?" Nodding his head towards Mikey's living room.

Mikey simply said, "Yeah," and invited him in.

"I got us a good deal." Colin whirled upon entering the flat. "Have you got a crusher?" he asked.

"A what?" Mikey responded. Confused.

"Something to crush the stuff up with?" Colin answered and looked around. "This will do," he concluded. Picking up a wooden spoon from the kitchen work top. All the apartments in the block were open plan. So, it was easy to move from living room to kitchen and vice versa.

Colin crushed the powder in both of the bags and continued. "Good to have a livener before we set off. Gets you in the mood," he informed him taking a hit from one of the bags. "This one is yours," he handed over a small bag of powder to Mikey. "Take it easy with it. I know you're not that experienced. Don't blow your load on it too soon."

"I won't," Mikey assured him. Picking up a key to take a hit. The same rush as the previous experience hitting him soon afterwards.

They walked out onto the street a couple of minutes later and turned right this time. They had to stop off at the Nationwide cash machine, next to Yates. So, Mikey could pay Colin back for the goodies.

They entered the Knowsley, got themselves a drink and found good seats near the big screen. The game would be kicking off in around twenty minutes time. They managed to fit in another round of drinks and a hit apiece before the match started.

Mikey didn't pay much attention to what was going on with the football. His head was as high as a kite. Enjoying his goodies and beer he listened to the United contingent, which Colin was amongst bemoaning their manager, David Moyes who had succeeded long serving manager, Sir Alex Ferguson, the previous summer who had retired. Things had not gone to plan, however. The United supporters sat in the pub; couldn't see how he would not now be sacked. There was no possible way he could survive. They had just been humiliated 3-0 at home by their biggest rivals.

Mikey was amused at how seriously they took this and how vicious they got about it.

Colin was beside himself with the result. He concluded that he and Mikey should just get pissed to drown their sorrows.

After a few more pints and hits, Mikey started to drone on to Colin about his time with Tanya. How after they spent the night together, she now didn't seem interested. Colin told him. "Fuck her, mate. There's plenty more around. If she doesn't want to know, forget her."

"I really like her, though," Mikey protested.

"Maybe she just wanted a fuck," Colin told him. "Some girls are like that."

Mikey knew that wasn't the case and shot back. "I don't think so. She wants us to spend time together. Wants us to take it easy and get to know one another. Slow things down. Then see where it leads us."

"You're too young to be settling down," Colin informed him. "You're not even thirty yet. You need to be out enjoying yourself. Living the good life. Take a different girl home every weekend, show her a good time. Then fuck her off in the morning. Don't let them cramp your style."

Mikey was somewhat infuriated by this analysis, but he kept his feelings to himself. He knew he shouldn't treat Tanya that way. Or any other woman for that matter. If that was Colin's view on it and was how he operated. Then that was his choice and no business of his. "I will just see how it goes," was all he said.

"Good lad!" Colin encouraged. "Now, let's go join in with those lads singing over there."

There was a group of five men near the pool table, with United shirts on. Singing football songs and clowning around. Mikey didn't know the words to any of the songs, though tried his best to fit in. A sudden urge came over him then. He said loudly to the group. "I've got one for you!" And began to sing.

"We pray to the God of tits and beer tits and beer, tits and beer."

"We serve him well!"

"We serve him well!"

"We serve him well!"

"We serve him well!"

"We pray all day and drink all night! And we serve him well!"

"Where did you learn that?" one of the men asked.

"Just made it up," Mikey told him.

"It's brilliant," The man said. "Let's do it again. All of us this time."

Everybody joined in the next time. After about four tries, they managed to get all the words right. Before they knew it, most of the guys in the pub were singing along.

Renditions went on for some time with, people coming over to Mikey to clap him on the shoulder or shake his hand. Congratulating him on a fantastic song.

The beer flowed and a good time was had by all. It did get a little rowdy, but no fighting broke out and it simmered just under the level of acceptability. It was well past midnight when he and

Colin walked back with their arms around each other, singing what now had become known as "The Tits and Beer Song." To their apartments. Wishing each other a good night on the landing and embracing. Mikey was revelling in what he had achieved, and sleep did not come until well past five that morning.

Chapter 16

Mikey shot out of bed at just after eight thirty the next morning. Having snoozed his alarm up until that point. He seemed to have an abundant amount of energy. As he quickly made his bed and got dressed. He decided to forgo his usual shower, as there wasn't the time. He raced down the stairs and entered the street. The adrenaline still flowing, as he desperately didn't want to be late. Laughing to himself. "Seany boy. It's nearly nine o'clock. Going to shout at me?"

He arrived at the shop with two minutes to spare and instantly locked eyes with Beth. "Are you okay?" She immediately asked.

"Yeah." He replied. "Just got up late, is all."

"Okay." Beth spoke. "Sean isn't here yet. But Siobhan is in her office. Just get to your desk quickly."

"I will. Thank you." He thanked her. Walking at speed towards the back office.

"Good afternoon," Rachel laughed.

"Good morning," was all he replied. Trying to keep his voice as level as he could. He surprisingly didn't feel all that tired from the previous evening. He felt in those moments, like he could easily have carried on the party. "Good morning, Liang," he added whilst firing up his laptop.

"Good morning, mate," Liang quietly replied.

"Look what the cat dragged in," Rachel taunted.

"Good job Sean isn't here."

"I just didn't get much sleep last night," Mikey shot back.

"Out drinking again, were we?" Rachel mocked.

"No," Mikey quietly answered. "I was just tossing and turning all night. So, I would appreciate it if you just left me alone."

"Don't you speak to me like that!" Rachel furiously fired back.

"Why? Does it offend your ego?" Mikey sarcastically enquired.

"What's gotten into you lately?" she lambasted him. "Your attitude is going downhill."

"You! You fucking bitch!" is what he thought. "Nothing," was all he said.

"You're behaving differently towards me lately." She spoke. Calmer now.

"Don't let her control the narrative," he told himself.

"The awakening of the soul is a most prized commodity," he told her.

"What are you talking about?" Rachel laughed at him.

"When you decide to be yourself the universe opens to your beliefs," Mikey informed her. Not sure where he was going with this. But it made sense in his head.

"Have you been reading one of your crappy philosophy books again?" she probed with a sense of loftiness to her voice.

"No book is crappy. You should try educating yourself sometime," he shot back.

"How dare you!" she bolted with fire in her eyes.

"I didn't mean to offend," Mikey protested. Showing her his open palms as a gesture of peace. "It's just that wonderful knowledge can be found in books."

"You think you're so much better than everybody else, don't

you?"

"Not at all."

"Going out drinking the night before you have work, is not acceptable."

"What are you going to do? Grass me up?"

"No. I wouldn't do that."

"I know. We're a team here, aren't we?"

"Yes. We are."

"So, Sean or Siobhan will never know about any of this, will they?"

"Not from my lips they won't."

"Perfect. I've got you on toast," Mikey thought to himself. He spoke, "I'm glad to hear that."

"There's no need for your attitude, though," she retaliated.

"I'm not trying to have an attitude," he innocently spoke back, "I just want to get on with my job."

"You've changed," she informed him. "I don't like it. What's happened to the sweet boy I used to know?"

"I'm still the same," he assured her feeling a stab of pain come over him all of a sudden. He urged himself to reconcile. Perhaps he had gone too far. Rachel wasn't all bad after all, was she? She had her good points about her, and he looked at her in that moment and felt sorry for her. He didn't know why he did. She just looked so helpless with the way he was behaving. "I'm just trying to be a better person," he quietly told her.

"Have you been hanging around with a new group of people?" she asked.

"No." He instinctively lied. Wanting to protect himself.

"Right," Rachel quietly noted. "I just don't need you giving me a hard time right now. I've got too much going on. I've already told you, I'm in the process of moving. I don't need your bullshit on top of the stress I already feel."

"You actually had me going for a minute there," he spoke to himself. "But it really is all about you. Isn't it?" He just simply replied, "Okay." Thinking it best to leave things as they were, for the moment.

"When you two have quite finished," Tariq suddenly chipped in standing in the doorway. "Beth is dealing with a customer out there. We can hear every word."

"Sorry, Tariq," Rachel apologised.

"Sorry," Mikey mumbled.

"Just keep it down," Tariq instructed. Looking at Liang for a long moment who just nodded his head. He then turned and left the room.

"I need a coffee," Mikey announced. Getting up from his desk.

Once he had left the room. Rachel turned to Liang and sarcastically spoke, "Thanks for your support there."

"What do you mean?" Liang innocently asked. "Are you for real?" Rachel hotly asked.

"I thought you had it under control," Liang protested.

"I did," Rachel confirmed. "I can handle that little dweeb all by myself. A little back up wouldn't go amiss, though."

"I would have stepped in, if he had gone too far," Liang assured her.

"He's getting a bit cocky," Rachel commented lost in her own thoughts and almost oblivious to her companions' reassurance. "Do you think it's Beth's influence?" she then asked.

"Probably," Liang confirmed. "And he's gotten very pally with Tariq, as well."

"Tariq?" Rachel asked. "What's he been saying?"

143

"He gave me some shit about how I've been treating Mikey," Liang told her.

"What did you say?" she quizzed.

"Not much," he confided.

"Seriously?" Rachel condemned. "Can you not stick up for yourself?"

"He just caught me off guard," Liang protested. "I will be prepared for him, if he tries it on again."

"I see it now," Rachel declared. "I bet he's told him to have a word with you. He's too much of a shit bag to do it himself, so asked Tariq. The little worm. Knowing that Tariq thinks he's big and hard. Dragging your name through the mud. We haven't done anything wrong and he's trying to destroy our reputations with our colleagues."

"Do you think it would be best if we just laid off him for a while?" Liang almost pleadingly asked.

"Not one bit," Rachel shot back. "He's the one that's a little snake. Trying to discredit the ones who actually work hard for this company. He's not interested in anything but himself. You can tell by the way he just saunters about the place. Hardly even speaking to anybody. Thinks he's bigger and better than everybody else. Now he's got that little midget, Beth. He's coerced her into believing his crap. And now Tariq. He's trying to turn everybody against us, and we can't let him."

"How long does it take to make a cup of coffee, anyway?" Liang interjected.

Mikey had been a while in the kitchen. That was due to the fact Beth had engaged him in conversation.

"What's going on?" she asked him.

"How do you mean?" he enquired.

"You clearly went out last night," Beth told him.

"Not you as well," Mikey rebuked.

"I'm trying to help you," Beth fired back.

Sensing he had just hurt her with his comment. Mikey pleaded. "I'm sorry. I shouldn't have said that. You're right. I did go out last night and I'm feeling a bit fragile today. I'm sorry for the way I just spoke to you. You don't deserve it."

"It's okay," she reassured him. "Just don't make a habit of it."

"I know you said to only drink at the weekend, but I couldn't help myself," he protested.

"You have to control yourself," Beth comforted him. "The good thing is, is that you made it in today. At least you won't need to have any further awkwardness on that front. If you do find yourself needing a release when you have work the next day. Make sure you get home in time to sleep well enough to get here. I don't condone you going out when you have to be up. But if you must. Then be sensible about it."

"I spent the night with a friend." Mikey suddenly declared.

"Ohhhh, really." Beth enthused. Feeling more joyous upon hearing the revelation. "So, that's why you're tired." She laughed.

"Yeah." Mikey grinned.

"What's her name? And where did you meet her?" Beth quizzed. Her eyes gleaming with excitement.

"She's called Tanya and she works in the White Lion." Mikey informed her. "I met her after her shift on Saturday and we spent the night at mine."

"Check you." Beth beamed. "Keeping her with you for the whole weekend. Were you that good that she didn't want to leave?"

"No," he lamented. "She left on Sunday afternoon. She was

working the night shift, you see."

"So that doesn't explain why you're hungover today." Beth informed him. With a more serious tone to her voice.

"I told you I went out last night," he reminded her. "I went to the Knowsley with a neighbour of mine."

"So, you did," she conceded. "I was just trying to make sure you weren't trying to deceive me. Friendship is built on mutual trust. If we don't have that. We have nothing," she told him.

"I wasn't. I promise," he vindicated himself. "I was just excited to tell you about Tanya."

"I believe you," she declared. Excited again. "So, have you text her since?" Beth asked.

"No. Not yet," Mikey declared.

"Mikey!" Beth shot. "Why the hell not? It's been ages. She's going to be thinking you're no longer interested."

"She told me that we needed to take things slowly," Mikey protested.

"That's all well and good," Beth told him, "but that doesn't mean radio silence. Promise me you will text her today."

"I will," he promised. "I will text her when I get home."

"Good," Beth declared. "Don't go getting too clingy though. If she wants to take things slowly, you need to give her space. But not too much. You need to find the right balance."

"Wow! This is complicated," he announced.

"Just be natural," she taught him. "If you ever get stuck and need advice. Come to me and I will help you."

"Thank you. I appreciate that." Mikey genuinely and warmly thanked her.

The day got harder for Mikey the further it went along. He strangely felt worse as it wore on. The adrenaline of the morning was replaced by lethargy, as the afternoon rolled on. All he wanted to do was sleep. Every minute felt like an hour, and he was constantly clock watching. Thankfully, Rachel and Liang seemed to be wrapped up in their own conversations to pay much attention to him. She was showing him all the new furnishings she was getting for her apartment. Sean was not to be seen all day and Siobhan was busy in her office. He was thankful for these small mercies. "Never again," he said to himself. "No more drinking and taking that shit, on a school night." He had gotten away with it this time. Next time, he might not be so lucky. He endeavoured to restrict that type of thing, to a Saturday night. When he could relax all day on the Sunday.

Tariq joked with him as much when they closed the shop for the evening. Declaring. "Do it on a Saturday, mate."

"I will try," Mikey pledged to him.

"Until tomorrow, then," Tariq spoke.

"See you tomorrow," Mikey confirmed.

When Mikey entered his apartment he longed for his bed. He instantly made his way there. He remembered his promise to Beth and text Tanya. "Hey, how are you?"

"I'm good. How are you?" was her reply.

"Good, thanks," Mikey started with and couldn't think of anything else to say, so pressed send.

"I thought you had forgotten about me," Tanya replied.

"Not at all. I would never do that. Just had work today."

"I'm glad to hear it. I'm free Saturday."

"Maybe we could get something to eat? When you finish?"

"Sounds good to me. Just not fish 'n' chips. Haha."

"Great. And definitely not fish 'n' chips. What do you like?"

"Surprise me."

"Okay."

"See you Saturday."

"See you Saturday."

"Good night x."

"Good night x."

Mikey contentedly drifted off to sleep after that exchange. He did wake himself nervously a couple of times in the night, to check for any further messages from Tanya. Which there weren't. A night long, peaceful sleep. Came upon him just after ten.

Chapter 17

"So, what happened with Tanya? Did you text her?" Beth immediately quizzed Mikey upon seeing him the next morning.

"Yes. I did," Mikey declared, "we're going to have something to eat together on Saturday."

"Brilliant." Beth passionately brought her hands to clap together. "Are you meeting her after she finishes work?" she asked.

"Yeah," Mikey confirmed. "I don't know where to take her though. She's a vegetarian."

"McDonalds is off the cards then," Tariq joked. Joining in the conversation.

"Tariq!" Beth playfully punched him on the shoulder.

"Just jessing with you," Tariq affirmed. "I'm pleased as punch for you, mate."

"Cheers mate." Mikey smiled.

"You need to think of somewhere that's nice." Beth told him. "Atmosphere is important. Don't worry too much about the place having meat on the menu. Most places nowadays, have lots of vegetarian options. So, picking a place she will be comfortable and where you can communicate properly is what you should aim for."

"Yeah, I need to look for something suitable," Mikey agreed.

"Remember, atmosphere and making her feel comfortable. They're the most important things," Beth spelled out for him. "Remember what I told you about being natural. If she sees the

real you, there's no way she won't fall head over heels for you."
She beamed.

"She's right, Mikey," Tariq agreed. "If you be yourself and make her feel comfortable, she will be like putty in your hands." He grinned.

Beth shot Tariq a quick look, to tell him not to bring the tone down too much before Mikey spoke, "Cheers, guys. I appreciate your help. I hope it works out."

"You will be fine," Beth reassured him.

"Yeah, you will smash it mate," Tariq confirmed. "As you know, I've got the rest of the week off, after this morning. So, I want to hear all about it when I'm back on Monday."

"I will tell you everything," Mikey promised. "I want to hear about London, as well. When you're back."

"Yeah, should be fun." Tariq ratified. "Not seen the family down there for a while. So will be nice."

"Is Alicia going with you?" Beth asked.

"Yeah, she's more excited than I am," Tariq told her. "I'm sure my family love her more than they do me." He laughed.

"I wonder why?" Beth jibed.

"What's all the kafuffle?" Siobhan suddenly appeared and asked.

"Mikey's got himself a date," Beth joyfully responded.

"Really?" Siobhan dully replied.

"Tanya is her name. Mikey's going to wine and dine her, on Saturday night. Such wonderful news," Beth excitedly told Siobhan.

"Quite," Siobhan replied. "Tanya is the name of my son's ex-wife. Brings back awful memories."

"I'm sure this Tanya is much better," Beth flatly told her.

"Perhaps," Siobhan nonchalantly replied. "Now, I believe it

is work time."

"That's what we're here for." Beth smiled back.

Siobhan gave her a long glance, before walking up to her office.

"Don't worry about her," Beth told Mikey. Once Siobhan had disappeared. "You just concentrate on your date."

"I will and thank you." Mikey grinned.

"Anytime," Beth confirmed. Smiling back.

"Reggie's coming in this afternoon, anyway," Tariq chuckled to Mikey. "Shame I won't be here to see round two."

"Who's Reggie?" Beth asked.

"The new electrician," Tariq informed her. "He and Siobhan had a bit of a ding dong, the last time he was here."

"This I have to see." Beth laughed.

"I will be relying on you to tell me all about it," Tariq told her.

"I will be sure to," Beth confirmed.

Mikey started his morning work inwardly delighted with himself. Save for Siobhan, the day had been highly satisfactory so far. Rachel and Liang were strangely quiet. Save for a good morning and a few brief discussions about orders, they had hardly spoke. To him or to each other. "Has there been an argument?" Mikey mused to himself.

Due to the whirlwind nature of the days since Sunday, he had not had the time to think over his actions on that day. The quietude of the workplace now gave him that opportunity. He thought about the song he sung in the pub. "Bloody hell," he remembered to himself. He knew it could have been so embarrassing. But it wasn't. The other guys revelled in it. He was the centre of attention. He liked it. He had to admit. They were singing along with him. Clapping him on the shoulder and shaking his hand. None of it was planned. It was just spontaneous, and it worked. Not like him at all. It was exactly what that type of crowd enjoyed. A boisterous lad anthem, that was easy to sing along to. He smiled to himself when he realised, he actually fit in that day.

"I've come to fix your little spotlight issue," Reggie told Beth. Upon entering the shop.

"Ahhh, you must be Reggie," Beth politely replied.

"I can see my reputation goes before me." Reggie grinned.

"I only heard the good things, I swear," Beth preened.

"Clever one you, aren't you?" Reggie warmly complimented. Beth innocently smiled back.

"Where's the old crow?" Reggie asked.

"If you're referring to Siobhan, she's in her office," Beth courteously informed him.

"Ha-ha! You knew who I meant!" Reggie laughed.

Beth couldn't help but giggle and told him, "I will let her know you're here."

A couple of minutes later, Siobhan walked down the stairs and immediately engaged Reggie in conversation. "Hi, Reggie. What we need to do today is, those two spotlights near the front entrance keep short-circuiting. So, we need to fix them. Replacing them is probably not needed."

"Not only are you the finest manager in the land. You've now become the finest electrician ever to grace the earth," Reggie mocked her.

"How dare you speak to me like that!" Siobhan fired back.

"No need to get your knickers in a twist," Reggie explained. Smiling his gap-toothed smile. "I'm only complimenting you on your wonderful abilities."

"It didn't sound like that," Siobhan contested.

"Unfortunately, words can be misunderstood," Reggie calmly told her. "Especially from a guy like me. Who is not as educated as somebody like yourself. My brain doesn't have the capacity to understand, you see."

"Well, do you think you can fix them?" Siobhan asked.

"I don't know," Reggie answered. "I haven't looked yet. I will do so now and decide if they need replacing."

"They won't need replacing," Siobhan insisted.

"As the professional, I will decide that for myself," Reggie informed her. "There's no need to worry yourself any further. I have it in hand. You will have spotlights fit for Hollywood when I'm done. You can go back to being the best manager in the world."

"Just let me know when you're done," was all Siobhan said in return. Her eyes burning.

It turned out the spotlights did need replacing. Which Reggie efficiently did, and Siobhan was not happy about it. He left his invoice on her desk and told her, "Tell the boss man to ring me if he has a problem." Before promptly leaving the shop.

The silence in the back office was broken mid-afternoon when Rachel asked Mikey. "So, who's this girl you're taking out?"

Mikey took a moment to think of his reply. He eventually turned his face away from his screen and spoke. "Tanya, she's called."

"Where did you meet her?" Rachel asked.

"She works in the White Lion." Mikey responded.

"So, you met her when you were drunk?" Rachel mocked. "I don't drink. I was having a shandy." Mikey lied.

"Shandy, my arse!" Liang suddenly flew in. Which took Mikey by surprise. "I've told you before. I only drink shandy." Mikey reiterated.

"You're such a little liar," Rachel cut in. "How do you

explain yesterday's hangover then? I'm dying to know."

"I had a few. It's no crime," Mikey protested.

"It is when you think you can lie to us," Rachel fired back.

"I never lied. I told you yesterday, that I had a hangover," he reminded her.

"Yeah, then tried your best to cover it up," Liang interjected.

"Wouldn't you do the same?" Mikey asked.

"I wouldn't care," Liang volleyed back.

"He likes to live in his own world. Thinking he's better than everybody else," Rachel told Liang.

"Hasn't got Tariq to protect him now though, has he?" Liang observed. Looking directly at Mikey.

"What do you mean?" Mikey asked.

"Don't pull the innocent!" Rachel bolted. "You had Tariq have a go at Liang. Telling him to leave you alone. What's wrong? Not man enough to fight your own battles?"

"I don't know what you're talking about," Mikey disputed. Feeling the sweat drip from his every pore. He was getting nervous now. He had not felt this agitated in some time. He felt compelled to run away. "Stay! Stay and fight your corner!" he shouted to himself, through his mind.

"Haven't got the grapefruits, have you?" Liang taunted. "Just go running off to Tariq, won't you?"

"No! No, I won't!" Mikey tossed back. "I've got bigger grapefruits than you will ever have!" He was standing up over Liang's desk now.

Liang rose, and they stood toe to toe, looking at each other. "What's going on?" Sean demanded.

"Just a little misunderstanding," Rachel explained. "Boys being boys, is all."

"I came in here to find somebody to cover Tariq on the front desk and I find World War Three is kicking off!" Sean seethed at his employees. "I think it will be best if you, Mikey. Work at the front of the shop for the rest of the week. Where I can keep a better eye on you."

"It's not me you should be keeping an eye on though, is it?" Mikey shot back. Before he could stop the words leaving his lips.

"Oh, yes, it is!" Sean vehemently told him.

Mikey did work the rest of the day with Beth, at the front of the shop. It was made completely unbearable as Sean decided to move his laptop down and sit at the front counter, for the remainder of the afternoon. The atmosphere was tense and not many words were spoken. To make matters worse, it was quiet, and customers were fleeting. Both he and Beth busied themselves replenishing stock and displays, the best they could. They both felt a palpable relief when the day ended. Rob had come to pick Beth up, so there was no chance for any communication between them upon leaving. She did; however, manage to give him a sympathetic glance.

Mikey diverted to Tesco on his way home. He bought eight cans of Carlsberg, instead of four. He needed them tonight. He neglected to have any food and started drinking after he cooled a couple of his purchase, in his freezer for ten minutes. He was livid. How dare they speak to him like that. What did Liang mean about Tariq?

He hadn't asked Tariq to do anything. If he had. He had done it himself and Mikey had nothing to do with it. He needed to speak to Tariq. Not now though. He was on holiday. He would do so when he was back in work. "Fuck 'em! Fuck 'em all!" He denounced them as the drink took over. The insults got worse, the more he drank.

Chapter 18

Mikey had exchanged numbers with Mr Jefferson the last time they met. Mr Jefferson called him on Thursday evening to see if he was free on Friday. To have a drink and give him chance to read Mikey's poems. Mikey confirmed he was and, they agreed to meet at Tompsons Chippy. Which was only a short walk up the road from Energy Records. They met there after Mikey had finished work.

Mr Jefferson had with him a carrier bag filled with beer for the both of them. "I've come prepared," he joked with Mikey, upon seeing him.

They met outside the chippy rather than the shop as they thought it best to keep their meetings from Mikey's colleagues. Not that they had anything to hide. Mr Jefferson just thought it would cause unnecessary friction for his cohort should anybody start asking questions. He also knew what he had previously told Sean about Mikey's absence. So, it was best to keep a lid on things, for now.

They made the short walk down the Rock to Mikey's apartment. He had paid for the fish 'n' chips, in return for Mr Jefferson buying the beer. The communal door at street level flung open, as Mikey tried to put his key in. There stood Colin. "Mikey! My old mucker." He immediately embraced him.

"How are you, Colin?" Mikey asked. A bit taken aback.

"On top of the world," he announced. "Great night on Sunday."

"Yeah, it was fun," Mikey agreed.

"What you up to?" Colin queried. Looking at the bags the other two were holding.

"We're just going to have a quiet one. Eat our food and have a couple," Mikey told him.

"Good stuff," Colin enthused. "See you over the weekend. If you're out?"

"Yeah, probably," Mikey somewhat agreed.

With that, Colin shook Mikey's hand and nodded to Mr Jefferson. Before making his way off up the street.

When they entered the apartment, and the door was closed. Mr Jefferson asked, "Who was that?"

"Colin," Mikey informed him, "my neighbour."

"Friendly with him, are you?"

"Not so much as that. We've just started going out for drinks together, occasionally."

"Ok. Just be a bit careful of that one," Mr Jefferson warned.

"He's all right," Mikey contested.

"It didn't appear that you thought so from your body language."

"He's not all that bad. A bit loud, maybe. But he's all right," Mikey rebuffed. He actually was changing his mind about Colin, somewhat. He had enjoyed his company when they had been together. He was feeling himself getting a little defensive about Mr Jefferson's questioning.

"I'm just not sure he's the sort you should be mixing with," Mr Jefferson insisted.

"Can we just drop it, please," Mikey fired back. With some of his agitation, now manifesting itself in his voice.

"Okay," Mr Jefferson placated. "Where are your plates?"

They ate their meal watching the news on the TV. Mr

Jefferson insisted on doing so. He always liked to watch the news whilst eating his meals. To keep abreast of events and goings on. There wasn't much by way of conversation, as he was taking everything in and storing the knowledge. Once it had finished and so had their meal, he immediately washed the dishes and left them on the draining board to dry.

"Do you always do that?" Mikey asked.

"Yes," Mr Jefferson calmly answered. "It was one of my final steps, in getting an orderly routine."

"I will add it to mine," Mikey confirmed. "I usually leave them for ages before I get round to washing them."

"Just makes your job harder, if you do that," Mr Jefferson replied. "All the left-over food and grease, gets stuck and is harder to clean. If you do it straight away, it comes off easily. As it has no time to stick," he taught him.

"Makes sense," Mikey agreed feeling a lot calmer now. And was a little guilty about how short he had been about the Colin incident earlier.

"What's with Sean sitting at the front counter?" Mr Jefferson asked. "When I was in yesterday, he had plonked himself there."

"I had a disagreement with Liang," Mikey relayed.

"I see," Mr Jefferson passed a beer to his companion and opened one himself. Then fell silent, to give Mikey the floor.

"I went out on Sunday night, with Colin," Mikey started. "It ended up being a late one and I turned up for work with a hangover. The morning was fine and then in the afternoon, after Tariq left. Both Liang and Rachel started on at me. Saying I try to cover up my hangovers and I need to grow a set of balls. Saying that I live in my own world and, I think I'm better than everybody else. Nothing could be further from the truth. I'm scared most of the time. I want to speak and communicate. But I don't know how. Rachel said that I got Tariq to have a go at Liang. Because of the way he had been treating me. I didn't. I didn't do anything of the sort. I lost it and squared up to him." He was rambling and getting emotional by this point. He stopped and stared at his companion. Pleading for help.

Mr Jefferson put an arm on his shoulder and calmly spoke. "It's okay. In the short time we've been getting to know each other, you've grown so much."

"How?"

"You wouldn't have even thought about standing up to Liang, a month ago. This time you did. Granted, you may have gone about it in the wrong way. But that doesn't matter. Learn from it and be better next time."

"I've wanted to say something to him for ages."

"I know and now you have," Mr Jefferson soothed. "Firstly. It appears that Tariq has been a good friend to you. The way I see it is, he gave Liang a warning as to how he was treating you. Most probably told him he wouldn't stand for it. He protected you, without telling you. He did that as he didn't want you to appear weak."

"If Liang started treating me better, which he did. Then I would think that I dealt with the situation by myself?" Mikey asked.

"Exactly," Mr Jefferson confirmed. "That way, you get the dickhead off your back and, Tariq can keep an eye on the situation. Make sure he doesn't get out of line again. All the while, you gain confidence by knowing you have control of the situation. He has done a very selfless thing for you."

"But he did start with me again."

"Yes. But only when Tariq wasn't there. It's very cunning. As if you go running to tell Tariq, it just confirms what he confronted you about. If you don't. He will have control of the situation again. Because you will try to avoid any further confrontation," Mr Jefferson spelled out.

"So, what do I do?" Mikey asked.

"You have to be smarter," Mr Jefferson told him. "You're a bright boy. Clearly very intelligent. But where you lack, is the politics and social savvy. Most people with a high intellect do. Others who are not so fortunate as you, have to make up for their shortcomings. You see, what is wrong with the workplace is, the most intelligent and gifted people, they don't get the promotions. Because they don't know how to play the game. They lack the politics. The not so clever ones are better at this. Which makes them clever in a different way. Though, not an honourable one. They advance because they know the right people to arse kiss and how to make themselves look good. They will take credit for other people's achievements if they can. Discredit anybody they see as a threat and make sure management see them as incompetent. The truth is, they are frightened of somebody like you. They know by all rights; you should be light years ahead of them. So, they play games to hold you back. They play them much better than you, as they're petrified of you. As that's their only weapon.

Take that away from them and they have nothing. Take Siobhan, do you know why she treats you the way she does?"

"No."

"Because she is also frightened of you," he told him. "She knows you could potentially do a much better job than her, in the position she holds. So, she is scared you will take it away from her. You see, if Sean knew what was really going on and, his head wasn't being filled with crap about you. He would understand that both you and Beth, were his best two employees. Tariq is

160

competent enough, but his heart isn't really in it. That's not a slight. He's a good guy. It's just the truth. Want to know why Siobhan likes Rachel so much and vice versa?"

"Yes."

"Because they can control each other. Siobhan knows Rachel isn't a threat and will want to stay on her good side. Because she is aware of her shortcomings. Whereas Rachel, knows she can manipulate Siobhan. Kiss her arse enough to play to her ego and get what she wants. Tariq is too easy going to care about any of this and has a genuine caring nature. Like the way he stuck up for you."

"I'm grateful to him for that."

"You can help him also."

"How so?"

"He is a very confident person, on the outside. He doubts himself, though. Doesn't believe he has the potential to go far in life. As a friend, you should help him with that."

"How?"

"Compliment his achievements. Coax him to strive for his goals. Don't be too obvious about it. So, he feels as though you think he's stupid. Just try to make him understand that with a bit of focus, he can do whatever he sets his mind to."

"I will help him, I promise."

"As far as Beth is concerned, she's a smart cookie. Will make an excellent psychologist one day. When she completes her degree. Like you, she is very intelligent. However, she is more aware of how to play the game than you are. You remember the day Siobhan found the mistake, that she thought you made?"

"Yes."

"Beth played the game perfectly. She told the truth. In a calm and rational way, that could never be disputed. There never could have been any comebacks for that. It infuriated Sean and Siobhan so much because it hurt their egos and, they knew they could do nothing about it. This is what you need to learn. Do that, then your waters will be much calmer. Just like Beth's. What you did wrong with Rachel and Liang is, you rose to the bait."

"What do you mean?"

"Liang would never have said anything to you whilst Tariq was there. So, they waited for him to leave before they goaded you. Hoping to get a response. Which they got. They won. I'm sorry to say. If you didn't rise to it and dealt with it in a calmer fashion, just like Beth did. You would have been the victor."

"Stick to the facts and don't let them twist your words?"

"Exactly! That is the way to counteract them. Don't rise to their shit. They want you to do that. So, it makes you look like the bad guy. Who's Sean blaming for that incident?"

"Me."

"Yes. Because all he saw, was you squaring up to Liang. You look like the one in the wrong. There is a way to resolve this situation, however."

"How?"

"What I want you to do is stand up to Liang in front of Tariq. Maybe, ask him if he wants to continue your conversation about grapefruits. Calmly though. When Sean or Siobhan isn't around. You initiate the confrontation. Make sure Tariq is not in the same room, though is within ear shot. That way you will appear strong. I bet Liang backs down and if he doesn't and things get rough. You can bet Tariq will intervene. It's a win, win situation. But he will back off. He's a bully. And bullies are cowards."

"What about talking to Tariq, to thank him for what he said?"

"I wouldn't. Make it look like you have done it off your own steam. He did it because he wanted to boost your confidence. So, this will let him know that it has. In turn, it will boost his also. Knowing that he has helped you."

"Sounds perfect."

"It is. Now, please let me read some of these lyrical joys of yours." Mr Jefferson smiled.

Mikey handed him an A4 writing pad, that was filled with what he considered his best work. Mr Jefferson began to read in silence. He came across one in particular, that caught his attention. Entitled, "The Lost Boy." He read, before asking,

Life's endless corridor A maze of a daze

In strange days we live One apologetic boy

In an unrepentant world

Of sin, to make him conform The badness takes over When the dirt is found

The games the boy plays He regrets with haste Upon seeing the face

Of his tormentor

The scrub of the tub The whack of the hand The belt is bracing

Perfection needs chasing

"What is this one about?"

Mikey instantly realised which poem he had read. He put his head in his hands. Let out a sob and wondered what to do. He finally answered, through his fingers. "The bad thing."

"The bad thing?" Mr Jefferson almost inaudibly enquired.

"Yes," Mikey returned. Still not looking up. "My foster father. He used to make me get in a boiling hot tub and scrub myself clean, if I came home dirty. If I was both dirty and late, I would get the belt and a fist, as well. He made my childhood a living hell.

He wanted me to be perfect. But I always got dirty. A dirty

boy! A dirty boy! I was a dirty boy, and nobody loved me. That's why my parents left me. That's what he told me. He told me he was stuck with me because he had to repent his sins. That I was his punishment. I had to lick any crumbs I spilt off the floor when I was eating. I had to be perfect. I had to please him. Do everything, so that he wouldn't hurt me. If I ironed my shirt for school and there were any creases, I would get the belt. I was so scared. So alone. I had nobody. I cried myself to sleep every night. Hoping that my parents would come and rescue me. But they never came. Nobody cared. Nobody loved me. Alone. Alone. I've always been alone. Nobody has ever wanted to know me. I dread coming back here from work every day. I'm scared that he may come back. Come back and hurt me again. Tell me I'm now a dirty man. A dirty man, who takes things too far! I need to get in that tub and scrub myself! Scrub myself! Scrub myself!" Mikey was shaking by this point, and he looked up to find that Mr Jefferson was crying.

"That should never have happened to you," he said finally. "I will make this right. I will make you whole again."

"Help me," Mikey sobbed.

"I will," Mr Jefferson promised.

"I just want to be normal."

"You're better than normal. You're a special boy. Everybody loves you."

"Most people think I'm strange."

"That's because they're strange. You're the normal one. You have a good heart and care about people. You want to make the world a better place. Most people are self-serving. You're different. You can make a difference. Your parents must love you."

"Then where are they? Why abandon me?"

"It must have been circumstances, beyond their control. There's no reason not to love you."

"I don't see how!" Mikey screamed. Uncontrollably shaking by this point.

"There, there," Mr Jefferson embraced him. "Everything will be okay. I promise you."

They both cried in each other's arms for some time. Mr Jefferson slept on Mikey's couch that night. He didn't want to leave him in such a state and wanted to make sure he was all right.

Chapter 19

Mr Jefferson did not leave the following morning. Until he consolidated that Mikey was going to be okay. Once he had done so. He left and told him that he would be in touch.

Mikey went to work that Saturday morning, with unusual feelings. On the one hand, he was horrified by the fact that he had told another living being about the bad thing. On the other hand, he was relieved that he had finally shared the burden with somebody else. He knew that he could trust Tom to keep the information to himself. Why was he so interested in him, though? He couldn't shake that nagging question. Did he have an ulterior motive? It didn't appear that way. He tried and tried to think of something he could possibly gain from the situation. Any advantage he could get by befriending him in this way. He couldn't think of anything. So, he began to second guess himself. Maybe he was just being paranoid. The one thing he could not shake; however, was the fact that the vast majority of people in his life, had taken advantage of him. In some form or another. Tom did seem to be different. Mikey felt a genuineness to him. They now shared a common bond, after last night's incident. He felt closer to him now. He was the man who he had shared his deepest secret with, and he didn't back away. Totally the opposite. He hugged and consoled him. Stayed in his flat overnight, just to make sure he would be okay. He began to feel guilty about having these negative thoughts about him now. He had helped him when most would have turned away and run. Or worse still, mocked him. Told him that it was a long time ago and he needed to get over it. "That's the attitude of most people, isn't it?" he asked himself walking past the McDonalds on the Rock. But perhaps, not Tom.

"So, where you taking her?" Beth asked to his back. Patting him on the shoulder, as he was lifting the shutter.

"Picnic," Mikey suddenly decided. The thought had never occurred to him, until that moment. He had no clue as to where the idea came from. It just felt like the right thing to do. "The weather is going to be good today. So, I'm going to grab some stuff after work. Then take her down to Burrs for a peaceful meal." Burrs country park is the biggest park within the Bury area. Being situated close to the river Irwell. Which flows through the town. And being far enough away from the town centre. It made for a perfect setting for today's endeavours.

"Amazing." Beth enthused. "Such a great choice. It will just be the two of you there. Find a nice spot and it should be perfect."

"I think so." Mikey agreed. "Hopefully it's quiet today and Sean isn't around. That way, I can devise what I should buy."

"I will help you." Beth excitedly declared. "It should be just the two of us at the front today. I overheard Sean and Siobhan yesterday. Discussing a meeting with some prospective new band today. They should be busy with that. What are you thinking?" she asked.

He thought about his response for a few moments and then declared. "BBQ."

"Interesting." Beth thoughtfully replied. "Though, she is a vegetarian," she reminded him.

"I know." He confirmed. "She told me last time we were together, that she eats meat substitutes. Like Quorn and things. So, I was thinking. Get some Quorn sausages and burgers. Throw in some muffins or bread to go with. Maybe a bit of fruit and the job is a good 'un."

"Don't forget the cheese," Beth told him.

"And the sauces."

"I don't know what sauce she likes?" he admitted.

"Keep it simple. Just get ketchup, mayo and maybe some light mustard. Not the strong English stuff," Beth reeled off. "I will make a list for you. Go to Tesco after work and make sure you don't forget anything," she declared scurrying for a pen and paper. "Let's keep it to ourselves," she added upon seeing Rachel and Liang enter the shop.

"Ok," was his simple response.

Rachel and Liang, both gave them a polite, if somewhat formal. "Good morning," before heading off to the back office. Mikey felt thankful that he wasn't going to be working there with them today. He had far more important things to be worrying about than their games. He had been petrified the first afternoon on the front desk. Sean sitting there had made it even more uncomfortable. As the week wore on; however, he began to feel less nervous. He had newfound confidence about him, and he was displaying it, somewhat. He still felt a little anxious and at times, intimidated by a customer walking up to the desk. The positive was, he no longer felt the excruciating, overwhelming fear. He felt more in control of his body. He didn't need to stop himself from shaking, half as much. He felt proud of how far he had come.

But he knew that he still had a long way to go.

Mercifully, it was not busy that day. He and Beth had the time to outline exactly what he needed to purchase. Well, Beth mostly. She was incredibly excited by the prospect of Mikey making good on his potential with Tanya. She outlined the complete meal plan. Adding in some chocolates for a treat. She informed him that she wanted a full breakdown of how it went on Monday morning. To which he sarcastically replied. "Yes, Sergeant." Giving her a salute.

"Don't," Is what she shot back. With a look that told him, his attempts at humour were not appreciated.

He instantly quietened with this and replied. "I promise I will tell you all about it. And thank you for all your help. It means a lot to me." He thanked her. Genuinely.

"You're welcome," she replied. "Remember to just relax and be yourself. If she sees you for who you truly are. There is no way she won't fall for you." She smiled.

"I will. I promise," Mikey assured her.

Beth smiled at that and turned to deal with the customer, who had just entered the shop.

Mikey managed to get through his working day painlessly and headed to Tesco. Rachel and Liang had hardly bothered with their colleagues that day. Which neither of them minded. He and Beth were actually relieved. As it gave them the time to plan Mikey's date. She wished him good luck one more time when he was closing the shop. Before heading off in the direction of home. She smiled as she looked in the direction of Burrs, on her way.

Mikey carried the full picnic basket which he had purchased, with him to the White Lion. There he met Tanya and she joked, upon seeing him. "Are we going on holiday?"

"Not quite." Mikey replied. "I was thinking a nice picnic down Burrs."

"How thoughtful." Tanya beamed. "That's very sweet. I finish in about ten minutes. Do you want a drink while you wait?"

"It's okay, Tanya," was Sue's voice. "You get off now. I will take over from here. You go and enjoy yourself."

"Thank you, Sue," Tanya exulted. "I will make it up to you."

"No need," Sue assured her. "Go and have fun."

"Thank you," Tanya repeated. Before linking arms with Mikey to leave the pub.

They sauntered down past the town's police station and searched for an idyllic spot, near the river. They didn't want to go as far as the caravan and motorhome park. Nor the Brown Cow pub. As that would be where the main body of people would be. Especially on a warm afternoon such as this. In a region notorious for its rain. They had fortunately, chanced upon a dry day. Seclusion and the quietude of their solitude was the goal. A place where they could enjoy each other's company and not be disturbed.

"Here's perfect," Tanya declared picking out a spot by the riverbank shaded by some trees. It lent an open view of the countryside beyond, with the river clearly visible in between. The surrounding trees offered protection from passers bye.

Mikey spread out the blanket he had brought from his home, for them to sit on whilst Tanya busied herself, unpacking the picnic basket. She revelled in what she discovered inside. Taking out the throw away BBQ and Quorn meat. She gushed, "This is quite the thing to do. You're a very thoughtful person. I'm impressed."

Mikey's heart began to flutter at that. He just smiled back at her. Unable to think of a reply. He finally broke the silence, by instructing. "Pass me the BBQ and the lighter fluid, please. I will get it lit. So, it's warmed enough for when we've prepared everything."

Tanya wordlessly handed him what he had requested. Then busied herself preparing the salad and other condiments.

They enjoyed their burgers and sausages. Followed by the apples and easy peeler oranges. They proceeded to lay on their sides, facing each other. Propped up by their elbows. Feeding one another the milk tray chocolates Beth had told Mikey to purchase.

"This was a really great idea," Tanya warmly told Mikey.

"I wanted to give us chance to talk," Mikey informed her. "Spend some quality time together and enjoy each other's company. I know most girls would prefer an expensive restaurant. So, I'm sorry if I let you down with not taking you to one."

"Not in the slightest," Tanya encouraged. "I much prefer this. We get to eat and drink at our leisure here. There's no time limit on when we're expected to leave and nobody around, but us." She smiled.

"I like it too," Mikey agreed.

"We have plenty of other times to go to restaurants."

"Build things up and take it easy."

"Exactly. This is utter perfection right now." She leaned in to plant a kiss on his lips.

"I want to do nice things for you," he told her.

"This is the nicest thing that anybody has ever done for me," she informed him.

"Did your ex-boyfriend ever do nice things for you?" he asked.

"Occasionally, yes," she had to admit. "Not often though. And nowhere near as sweet as this. He doesn't even come close to comparing to you. So don't worry about that."

"It's just that I don't have much experience with this type of thing," he confessed.

"Well, it doesn't show," she reassured him. "I've only had

one proper relationship myself. My ex was the first proper boyfriend I had. Straight from high school. I was besotted by him back then. He filled my head with dreams of how he was going to whisk me away to all the wonderful places in the world. How we were going to have a massive house in the country and live the good life. Once he knew he had me under his spell. That's when things changed. He became abusive. It was always name calling. Telling me that I was worthless, and he was the best thing that ever happened to me. That I would never be able to find anybody as good as him. I was young and naïve enough to believe him. As the years went by, the abuse got worse, and he tried to cut me off from my family and friends. Luckily, he never got violent."

"That's awful," Mikey eventually replied. Taking her hand into his, "I promise that I will never treat you that way. You are a wonderful and beautiful young lady. You deserve to be treated as such. I'm not going to make you any promises of a massive house in the country. But what I will say to you is, I will always treat you right and work hard to give you the best life we possibly can have. If our relationship gets that far."

"I can see that," she told him. "I grew up and learnt my lessons. I realised how to spot guys like him. I can see one a mile away now. You are not like that. You are kind and gentle. You have an aura about you that radiates warmth and love."

Mikey kissed her this time and spoke. "I'm going to really enjoy getting to know you."

"And I am you," Tanya confirmed. "Let's go in those bushes there," she then suggestively winked. "Bring that tea towel."

Mikey blushed but did what he was told. They entered the bushes and Tanya looked around. Seeing if anybody was about and whether they could be seen. Once satisfied, she took the tea towel from his hand and placed it on the ground. "How naughty is this?" She giggled. Dropping to her knees on the towel and taking him in her mouth.

"Yeah," Mikey gasped.

After a couple of minutes, with Mikey's moans getting louder, she teased, "Are you as naughty as me, though?" Looking directly up at him.

"Y, yeah," Mikey stammered.

"Prove it," she ordered. "Take me by that tree over there."

He did so. Hoisting her up and lifting up her medium length skirt before entering her. He was both exhilarated and nervous, as he thrust deeper inside her. Both their moans got louder as he climaxed, and they breathlessly kissed. Laughing all the while.

"Well, that was fun," Tanya joked when they lay back down on their picnic blanket.

"Quite unexpected. Though awesome," Mikey agreed.

She laughed at him and lay in his arms for some time. They stayed for a while longer, talking and having fun. Before Tanya beckoned, "Shall we go back to yours? I want you to do that to me again."

"Nothing would give me greater pleasure," Mikey delicately seduced back.

They made their way back to Mikey's apartment and proceeded to put away the remaining contents of their picnic. Then entered the bedroom. Where they made love twice more that evening.

In the still before the dawn. Mikey lay awake. Mesmerised by the beauty sleeping beside him. He slipped out of bed with an outrageous amount of care. He didn't want to wake her. He tiptoed into the living room and lit a candle by the coffee table, to write. He decided that he wouldn't show this to Tanya just yet.

He would wait a while. See how things played out and read it to her, in the perfect moment. He picked up his favourite pen and wrote,

The wonderous beauties within your soul. Have crept inside my heart

And the lids of your eyes

Make such sweet shadow, when closed

The symptoms from the stream Believe in what we dream

It seems we are too deep

For my heart to consider sleep

A migraine has come our way Such hurricanes, put to shame

A migraine has come our way Even desert plains, feel the wave

Such decadent grace, within your face As the light reflects on delightful eyes The moonlight on the beautiful sea Put to shame with your gracious ways

Courage envelops my beating heart Thundering passion in our restful still

A delightful smile, comes forth erstwhile So gentle, though blood runs wild

A migraine has come our way Such hurricanes, put to shame A migraine has come our way

Even desert plains, feel the wave

Fear not the outside fright Inside are delicious delights Penetrating my every whim The precious ocean we swim

The ease with which my heart sleeps tight Wrapped within your righteous ways Fallow fields made lush with crops

My unworthy soul awoken from its malaise

A migraine has come our way Such hurricanes, put to shame A migraine has come our way

Even desert plains, feel the wave.

Chapter 20

Mikey resisted the urge to seek out the pub that Sunday. After Tanya had left to get ready for her shift in the White Lion. He instead had an old school day by himself. He even ignored a knock at the door. Which he assumed was from Colin. Whereas in the past, this would have made him feel anxious and unloved. This time, he felt content. He was happy in his own company.

He watched the rain lash down outside from his front windowsill. He thought of all the times he had sat in this very spot and prayed for social interaction. He vividly remembered those lonely days. With nothing but his own thoughts for company. He wondered if there were others out there, experiencing similar? Whether there was somebody who right now, was staring out of their window. Monstrously hoping that one day company would envelop their much-maligned soul. Wondering whether anybody even cared about them? If anybody cared if they lived or died. Mikey knew there had been times. When he thought that if he were to die, nobody would care.

He would not be missed in the slightest. Everybody would just go about their business as usual. The most he would get about his life, would be a passing comment. Things had changed now, however. He now had people who cared about him and would miss him if he were gone. This gave him reason to live and not just exist. As he had done so previously. For reasons unknown to him, this scared him. He was afraid to hurt those people. To let them down in some way and disappoint them. He had spent all his life, up until this point, afraid because of other reasons. A different type of fear. One of seclusion and apprehension. These new feelings worried him more. Not for himself. Rather for Tanya and Tom and Beth. Perhaps even Tariq. He had shown him kindness recently. They seemed to him like the only good people on the planet. Not hurtful or vindictive in any way. Rather helpful and good hearted. There were others involved now, he knew. He must not let them down. The notion occurred to him, that life could just be a tornado of different types of fear, for everybody.

The rain abated around six p.m. and Mikey decided to go for a walk. He didn't want to go drinking. He wanted to put his headphones on and wander through the streets of the town. In order to take stock and weigh up where his life was heading. This was something he had always enjoyed doing and it had been a while since he had. He slipped on his blue Adidas trainers and thin waterproof jacket. Slipped his headphones over his ears and stepped out into the street.

He wandered left past the library to the end of Silver Street. He remembered the last time he had walked this way. It had been the first time he had steeled himself to go for a drink. His heart was racing in his chest back then. Lost in the frantic thoughts of his mind. The juggernaut of anxiety unrelenting. Telling him all manner of pitfalls that could become him. He realised that he had failed that night. He didn't manage to go for a drink. "Or was it failure?" he second guessed himself. Maybe that day happened for a reason. To teach him to be better next time. He actually had learned from the mistakes he made that night. The next time he had actively sought out social interaction, he had been successful. As he was a little less bold in his choice of venue. He went somewhere that would be less busy. Maybe that happened for a reason. As both Tom and Tanya frequented the place he ended up in. For different reasons. One drinks there and the other is employed. But still, he would not have formed a relationship with either. Had he not gone there. He would probably be still sat in his flat, alone. Dreaming that one day he could maybe find some company. If the lesson of his first failed trip, not been taught. Tom had told him in everything you do, think of one thing you could have done better. Then implement it next time. That was exactly what he had done. Before he had even been taught that lesson. So, perhaps he already knew? And just didn't know that he knew. "Instinct?" he asked himself. "What else do I already do, that I am unaware of?" he further quizzed as he reached the entrance for the market. He decided to sit upon the same bench, he sat upon the day he went to meet Tanya.

He now vividly recalled that day. How he had almost called the whole thing off. He was that petrified. The thought of having to see her that day made him feel physically sick. Not in a way that she repulsed him. Far from it. It was a nauseating fear of failure. He liked Tanya a lot. He knew that even then. He was desperate to make a good impression. Just absolutely terrified that he would mess things up, or she would think that he was an idiot. Think that there was no way that he would ever be good enough for her. See him for the bumbling idiot that he was. Make an excuse to leave, as he utterly bored her to death. The opposite had transpired, however. He had found her easy to talk to. After he got over his initial nerves. Which he knew she spotted in an instant. She coaxed him out of that, he realised. Engaged the conversation and made him feel at ease. Come out of himself and gave him confidence. He was astounded to realise that she was actually interested in him. Why else would she have done those things? Tanya was a pretty girl and could probably have any guy she desired. One where she wouldn't have to try hard to get him to talk to her. A guy with a smart mouth and funny jokes to make her laugh. She could just sit there and laugh it up. Enjoy herself, without having to put much effort in. "Have I found the one girl on the planet, that actually likes me?" He asked himself. Out loud.

There was nobody around to hear him. The market area was always deathly quiet, of a Sunday evening. With there being no stalls open for trade. Mikey knew now that he had made the right decision. Having gone to see her that day. He knew if he hadn't. He would probably never have forgiven himself. For a guy like him, that sort of chance doesn't come around very often. So, he had to grasp the nettle. Which he had and, he felt proud of himself. For having done so. He feverishly did not want to fail with her. "Don't be anxious and be calm about it." He calmed himself. "Learn to be better with Tanya. The same way you are with life."

The rain started its light patter once again, as he rose to walk back towards the bus station. He switched his music off at this point and decided to walk through. All the way round the curve that brought you to the other side. Where the entrance to go down the stairs, to the Metrolink platform was located. At the height of the curve, stood the disused toilets that were in operation for many years. He always felt eerie when near those toilets. As that was where pensioner Shirley Leach, had been murdered back in 1994. She had missed her connecting bus, on her way home from Fairfield Hospital. One of two hospitals that served the town at the time. The other, Bury General, on Walmersley Road had since been demolished, to make way for residential apartments. A visit to these toilets cost her her life. It was one of the town's most notorious unsolved crimes for many years. Until bus driver Ian O'Callaghan, was finally apprehended in 2006. Following an arrest for drink, driving.

When DNA taken was run through the police database, it matched that found at the crime scene. Mikey hurriedly scurried past.

He heard a commotion, as he reached the entrance for the Metrolink. He realised as he got closer, that it was a frail looking older man. He had a can of Carlsberg special brew lager in one hand and was rapping. Mikey listened to the raspy, throaty, hostile vocal.

Breakin' arms and legs All day, all night Breakin' arms and legs I've had my fights

They tell me I'm not right I don't need advice

Fuck you, it's my right Gunna flow all night

Breakin' arms and legs All day, all night Breakin' arms and legs I've had my fights

Breakin' arms and legs If you wanna fight

I'll break yours tonight I don't need your shite

Breakin' arms and legs If you wanna fight

I'll break yours tonight I don't need your shite

Breakin' arms and legs All day, all night Breakin' arms and legs I've had my fights

Mikey decided to quickly go back the way he had come. He was suddenly scared of this man. He looked and sounded like he was spoiling for a fight. He didn't want to give him any reason to start with him. He whirled past the toilets once again.

Proceeded to walk to the end of the station, where the crossing for the Knowsley stood. The thought of crossing and going in for a pint then entered his head. He stood and thought about it for a long moment. Before eventually deciding against it. He instead walked left and crossed further down the road. Turned right adjacent to the Town Hall and brought himself back onto the end of Silver Street. He walked past the library again, to his apartment. Quietly and delicately, he opened the communal door. If Colin was home, he did not want him to hear him enter. He silently closed the door and tiptoed up the stairs. Breathing a huge sigh of relief when he closed and locked his apartment door.

He poured himself a glass of orange juice and lay on his couch. He wanted to listen to some music. After pondering for some time, he decided to play some Bach. It was Tanya's favourite classical composer and he wanted to think of her while he listened. After a good half an hour of listening, he grabbed his phone and text her,

"Hey, hope your shift went well? X"

"See Beth. No radio silence this time," he mumbled out loud. Reassuming his leisurely position.

Chapter 21

"Yeah, bit quiet. But good. How was your evening, x?"

Was how the text back from Tanya read. When Mikey opened it the next morning, upon waking. They exchanged a few more texts. He told her of his walk the previous evening. Leaving out the part about the rapping drunk. They chatted pleasantly and arranged their next meeting for the coming Friday. Mikey proceeded to make his bed and set out his clothes for the day, on top of it. Hopped into the shower and prepared for work.

He walked down the Rock with a spring in his step. Despite the insistent rain, that had still not relented. He arrived at the shop at exactly the same time as Tariq. They greeted each other with a smile and Mikey asked. "How was London?"

"Boss, mate," Tariq enthused. "We had a blast. It was awesome seeing the family again. It's been too long. How has it been here?" he enquired. Opening the shop door with his key. With the shutters now fully up and secure.

Mikey remembered his conversation with Tom, about not letting on about what happened with Liang. He decided to honour that agreement. So answered, as they made their way to the front counter. "Brilliant, mate. I'm over the moon that you had a great time. It's been pretty quiet here. I worked on the front desk with Beth, in your absence."

"Really?" Tariq asked with surprise. "I thought Rachel would have jumped all over that."

"I did too," Mikey agreed. "But she had no say in the matter.

Sean came down and told me to do it."

"Ok," Tariq slowly articulated. "How did you find it?" he cautiously added.

"I actually enjoyed myself," Mikey admitted. "I was massively surprised. As I don't usually like dealing with the public."

"Yeah, you don't," Tariq agreed. Then grinned, clapped him on the shoulder and added. "Good to see you have more confidence about yourself. Check you. It's not always a bad thing that you keep yourself to yourself. But sometimes, having the confidence boost of interacting can only be a good thing. That's the way I see it."

"I agree," Mikey told his work colleague. "I feel my front desk experience was good for me. It gave me more confidence. Couldn't have done it without you encouraging me though. So thank you," he warmly and gratefully confided.

"Anytime, mate." Tariq beamed. "It's you who deserves the credit, not me. You made that step yourself."

"Wouldn't have done it without you pushing me," Mikey politely contested. "You're very good at motivating people. I've just thought that you love your gym work and boxing. You're good at motivating people. Why not study to become a personal trainer? I think it would suit you perfectly."

"Don't think I'm clever enough for that," Tariq lamented.

"Of course, you are," Mikey encouraged. "I think you would absolutely smash it."

"Cheers, mate," Tariq warmly thanked him. "I will certainly consider it." He then looked to the front door and saw Siobhan pulling down her umbrella. He added, "Best shush up. Here comes the dragon."

Mikey laughed and chipped in. "Tell me about it."

Tariq quickly and quietly spoke his next words. As to not let the entering Siobhan overhear, "Tell me later, what happened with her and Reggie. And more importantly, how it went with Tanya."

"I will," Mikey promised and mischievously grinned back. Before walking in the direction of the kitchen. Before long, he felt a presence behind him.

"Morning Mikey. Come up to my office when you're ready please," Sean somewhat coldly told his employee. Then instantly headed out of the room as Mikey was making himself a cup of coffee.

"Yeah, sure," Mikey replied. Feeling a pang of anxiety come over him. He finished making his coffee and decided to leave the finished product on the worktop. Rather than take it upstairs with him. He composed himself. Told his body and mind to remain calm. Before climbing the stairs to Sean's office.

He quietly knocked and was instantly told that he could enter. "Have a seat, please," Sean invited.

Mikey wordlessly took the seat offered. Directly in front of his employer. On the opposite side of the desk.

"I just want to talk about last week," Sean began. "I firstly want to tell you. Behaviour such as you displayed. Is unacceptable in my workplace."

Mikey kept his silence with this opening statement. Surprisingly, he was very still sat in his chair.

Sean assessed him with his eyes. Realising there was no response forthcoming. He continued. "This time, I am having an informal chat with you as I understand you have been under a lot of stress recently. Although, that doesn't fully excuse your behaviour. I want you to explain to me, why you thought it was okay to behave in that manner? And what you hoped to achieve?"

Mikey told himself to remain calm. Sean's words and tone had cut into him. His leg began to shake beneath the desk. "I, I don't believe I did anything wrong," he stammered. Feeling the sweat run down his back.

"How can you say that?" Sean asked incredulously. "You stood up in an aggressive manner to one of your colleagues," he reminded him.

"Only because he goaded me," Mikey contested. Feeling a little more confident in himself. He knew he couldn't just stay silent and drift through this meeting. He had to express himself. It took all his effort to keep his composure.

"In what way?" Sean quickly fired back.

"Both he and Rachel were winding me up," Mikey told him. "I know they were looking for a reaction and unfortunately, I gave them one. That's why I'm sat here now and not them." Mikey shot back. With more relish than he had ever spoke to his employer before.

"You're sat here now, because of your own behaviour. Not that of your colleagues," Sean told him in a stern, low voice that told his audience that he wasn't buying his explanation.

"You told me that I needed to stick up for myself more," Mikey reminded him. "That's all I was doing. Sticking up for myself and defending my corner."

"I struggle to understand how you would need to defend your corner?" Sean quizzed. "Rachel is a young female and Liang is brand new to this business…"

"You don't know what it's like…" Mikey cut in.

"Don't you ever dare have the audacity to interrupt me when I'm speaking, again," Sean angrily jumped back in. "The feedback from the other two colleagues you work with, is that you have a new bad attitude that they find distasteful. After the way you have behaved here, with me today. I can see where they're coming from. I've told you before that you need to buck your ideas up. That doesn't mean I want you fighting with your colleagues. It means I want you to get your work done and be polite to your colleagues," he raged. Then fell silent. Waiting for a response.

Mikey cowered back to what he had just heard. He wanted to run. He was getting overwhelmed with bad thoughts again. He was scared. Petrified. He willed and willed himself again, to fight it. To believe in himself and say what he was feeling. He desperately wanted to find the right words, to make Sean understand. He finally managed. "I just feel the way they speak to me sometimes, is not right."

"Listen to me, Mikey. And listen well." Sean leaned forward. More calmly now though still with a furious look in his eye, "Rachel has worked here for over two years. I have never heard a bad word said about her attitude by anybody else, in all that time. She is a young lady, and you need to learn to be a gentleman with her. The feedback I have received about Liang, is that he is hard working and has fit in well.

The only person I ever get negative feedback about, is you. Now, why is that?" he posed.

"Because you only listen to who and what you want to hear." The words slipping out of Mikey's mouth before he had chance to arrest their course.

"Excuse me?" Sean asked. With a quiet fury.

"All, all I mean is that I, I don't feel like you listen to me properly sometimes," Mikey somewhat stumbled back.

Sean leant back in his leather chair, beckoning him to continue.

Mikey did so. Knowing this had to be said. "I feel that

sometimes you don't see what people are really like. I mean, you don't see the other side to them. They suck up to you because you're the boss. Has it never occurred to you, that people suck up to you because of that? I would never do that. I'm different. I'm honest. You have to earn my respect. These are things you can no longer see, as perhaps you've become cocooned in your own world. I'm not saying these things to be insulting. I just want to make you aware, that I have an opinion too."

Sean stared at his employee in silence, for a couple of long moments. Taking in the incredible things he had just heard. Before finally speaking. "I am finding it increasingly difficult to help you here. I am going to put what you just said, down to the fact that you're under a lot of strain. I understand the impact that getting hauled into my office must have had on you. You're trying to defend yourself. I get it. On that basis, I am going to allow you to have the day off today. I want you go downstairs and leave immediately. Don't tell anybody why you're leaving. I will speak to them later. Then tomorrow, I want you to come in with a better attitude. And we will say no more on the subject. Now, please leave." He finished. Diverting his eyes to his laptop screen. To signify the conversation was at its conclusion.

Mikey silently left the office and went back downstairs. He saw Beth as he reached the bottom and quickly spoke before she had chance to. "Hi Beth, something's come up and I need to go home. I've squared it with Sean."

"Ok. Is everything all right?" she asked with concern written all over her face. "Yeah." Mikey answered. "I will talk with you about it tomorrow," he assured her.

"Okay." Beth nodded. "Take care and see you tomorrow."

"You too. See you tomorrow," he reciprocated. Beginning his walk to the door.

"Mikey," Beth called after him. When he turned back she was upon him and embraced him in a hug. When their bodies parted, she gave him a sympathetic smile and he went on his way.

Thunder rolled through Mikey's mind as he made his way back to his flat. The rain had thankfully decided to give the game up, for now. He made a detour to Tesco and picked up a twelve pack of Carlsberg. He needed a good drink tonight. His raging mind was beyond furious.

"Can you get me some goodies please, mate?" He text Colin on his way home from Tesco.

A couple of minutes passed, before he got a reply. "I'm working, pal. Bit early isn't it?" "I've had a fucker of a morning and need to get off my face."

"I know the feeling. I will ring my guy and verify you. Text you back in a min."

"Ok, thanks."

Mikey walked and waited for Colin to come back to him. As he approached Wyldes, he got one. "Ring the number I've just text you. Tell him Colin sent you to speak to Mr Bifter."

"Ok, thanks. Just getting to my flat. Will ring him when inside."

"No worries. Take it easy, man."

"Yeah, I will do. Cheers mate."

He walked up to his apartment and dumped his alcohol on the kitchen worktop. Picked up his phone and dialled.

"Hello."

"Hi, I'm Mikey. Colin sent me to speak to Mr Bifter."

"What you after?"

"Erm, I mean Colin sent..."

"I mean what do you want?"

"Oh, sorry. A fifty, if okay please?" "Where to?"

"Silver Street, please."

"Ok, I will call you when outside."

"Ok, thank you."

The phone on the other end went dead. Mikey sat there nervously waiting for the phone call. He turned his phone up to full volume. In order to make sure he didn't miss the call. He put his beer in the fridge and was then horrified to realise he needed cash to pay for his goodies. He rushed back out of his apartment and down the stairs. Jogged to the HSBC on the corner and went inside to use the cash machine. Unlike the Nationwide, there is no machine on the outside of the HSBC bank. So, the inside one can only be used during opening hours. He got his cash and jogged back. As he reached the top of the stairs, his phone rang.

"Hello?"

"Outside, on the side street. Next to Pizza Hut."

"Ok, coming now."

"Bye."

"Bye."

Adrenaline filled Mikey's stomach, as he crossed the road. Walked past O'Neill's bar and Pizza Hut and stepped into the side street. He locked eyes with a young-looking man, sitting inside a black Volkswagen polo, with tinted windows who beckoned him into the passenger seat. When Mikey had closed the door, he asked. "What you after?"

Learning his lesson, Mikey replied. "A fifty, please."

Wordlessly the man discreetly handed a bag to Mikey. Who gave over the cash in return.

"Thanks," Mikey spoke.

The young man just nodded, and Mikey got out of the car. He bounced back to his apartment, with a convulsing amount of nervous energy. The whole experience was utterly surreal to him.

He picked up the same wooden spoon Colin had used and proceeded to bash up the powder. Picked up a key and snorted a large amount up his nose. Grabbed one of his cans from the fridge and made his way to the couch. Put the first Spark Town album on his headphones and drank deeply.

He drank three of his cans and took two more hits, whilst listening to his music. When the album ended, he set his headphones aside and began to stare into the space in front of him. He gently rocked back and forth. As the anger swelled inside him. His eyes burned with rage.

"How fucking dare, they?" he violently said out loud. "They think they're so fucking clever. Playing games and messing with people's lives. I'm going to teach them all a fucking lesson. Who do they think they're messing with? I'm not that shit house that they used to know. Rachel thinks she can manipulate everybody. The rude narcissistic fuck! And Liang! The fucking prick! I might just take up boxing and put him back in his place. Fucking Siobhan! The up her own arse, condescending, arrogant little rat bag! Needs bringing down a peg or two. And fucking Sean! How can he not see what is going on? He's supposed to be an intelligent businessman. How can he be so blind? These fuckers are taking him for a ride. Licking his arse like, 'Oh, Prime Minister.' Then being horrible little bastards behind his back. Playing their politics.

Getting inside people's heads. Well, yes! They are inside my head. They think they've won! They have won the battle. But I won't let them win the war. I will be better than them. Teach them a lesson. Show them that they're total knob heads! The thick, insecure, little fuck heads. I am better than them and I will prove it!" He finished his rant. Then angrily threw his empty beer can, in the direction of the kitchen.

The anger did not run its course all day. The more he drank and sniffed. The worse it got. He took a lot of it out, by putting on some Metallica and other heavy metal bands on his headphones. He loudly sung along and jumped all over his apartment. He was not able to keep himself still. The combination of his feelings, alcohol, and drug intake, made it impossible to remain calm. He ignored three calls from Tom and also, his door buzzer. Which he assumed was from him also.

He finished off his stashes just after midnight and fell back onto the couch. He finally had time for calmer reflection. As his heart rate slowed. He began to weep and sobbed. "Why can't I just have a normal life? Why can't they all just leave me alone? Please, leave me alone and let me get on with my life. I'm different to you. But so, what? I may be more intelligent than you, but I don't think I'm better. I just want a happy life. I just want to be normal and left alone. Please stop picking on me. I can't take it anymore. Please leave me alone."

Mikey stared up at the ceiling for a good half an hour. Before finally taking his weary body off to bed.

Chapter 22

Mr Jefferson was waiting for Mikey on his street the following morning. He wanted to intercept him, before he went to work. He had been into Energy Records the previous morning. More to see Mikey, than to purchase a record. Which was always the case. Since the first time he had been in and saw him working there. Peering through into the back and noticing him, sat at his desk. Every time he had been back since, was in the hope that he would be there. And to hopefully engage him in conversation.

He had enquired of Beth, as to Mikey's whereabouts. She had been a little emotional, when informing him that he wouldn't be attending work that day. He had managed to get from her, with the strict assurance of confidentiality. The fact that it was Sean, who had sent Mikey home and he seemed upset about the whole ordeal. Mr Jefferson assured her that he would speak with him and make sure he was all right.

Beth had thanked him for this, and he left the shop.

He made his way to Mikey's Silver Street home and tried to call him. Three times in fact. Without success. He buzzed the buzzer, attached to the communal door at ground level. There was no answer there, either. This troubled him. He then remembered his neighbour. What was his name? Colin? Yes, that's it. Mikey said he lived in the apartment across the hall. It was only the two of them on that floor. So, if Mikey lived at number three. Then Colin must be at number four. He buzzed. No answer. "Fuck!" Mr Jefferson swore.

He decided to try back later and call when he got home. Even then, the young man he had gotten to know, seemingly did not want to be disturbed. He was extremely worried by this. Considering what he had told him about his childhood, the last time they met. He hoped he hadn't done anything stupid. That's what had brought him here this morning. He had to know that the young man was okay. He waited, with the rain pounding and soaking him to the bone. For the resolution of his fears.

Mikey appeared just after half past eight. "Mikey!" Mr Jefferson called to him.

A startled Mikey replied. "Tom?"

"Thank heavens you're all right." Mr Jefferson spilled out with relief. Studying his face. "I'm aware that Seany boy sent you home yesterday."

"Who told you that?" Mikey hotly asked.

"It doesn't matter. What matters is that you're okay. I thought you might have done something stupid." Mr Jefferson was more fidgety than Mikey had ever seen him be before.

That nagging question about why he was so bothered about him came back with a vengeance in that moment. "Why are you so bothered about me?" he fired at the old man.

Mr Jefferson was a bit stunned by this. He searched for a response. After taking a moment to compose himself. He replied. "Because I have made a lot of mistakes in my life and by helping you. I hope I can partly atone for some of them."

Mikey was not in the mood for any of this. He had a hangover, and his nose was on fire. He shot back. "You want to make yourself feel better, by helping me. Is that the way it is?"

"No," Mr Jefferson pleaded. "I'm doing it for you and only you."

"Well, I don't have the time now. I need to get to work."

Mikey coldly declared. Moving off in that direction.

"Mikey!" Mr Jefferson called after him. There was no response.

Mikey had woken up that morning, with even more fury inside of him. He despised the way he had been treated. As he walked to his workplace, he told himself to calm down. He had to put on a front and pretend. Nobody could see how he was feeling inside. He had to protect himself at all costs. He had to deal with the situation in a clever and calculating way. The people who had wronged him, had to pay. He could not let them get away with it. He took a few deep breaths to calm himself, before entering the already opened shop.

It was Sean who was inside. He was alone. "Good morning, Mikey," he greeted him.

"Good morning," Mikey reciprocated. "I'm feeling much more energised today," he instantly continued. Giving Sean no chance to interrupt. "Control the narrative and make him listen to what he wants to hear. The truth doesn't matter to him, so why bother?" he asked of himself. "I want to prove to you, that I am somebody who is worth employing. I want to show you my worth."

Sean's toothy grin appeared upon hearing those words. "That is music to my ears," he told him. "I want this business to run right and everybody in it, to pull in the same direction. To help it grow and make all of our lives, better. I can see that you have taken my words on board and come in today, with the right attitude. I was here early today, to make sure of that. I am now satisfied, that is the case. I have a meeting to go to, so I will let you open up as normal. I hope you continue to progress." He smiled again and nodded to his employee, before leaving the shop.

"Get on my toast, butter boy," Mikey thought. As he watched him saunter out.

"Hey," Beth softly spoke when she entered the kitchen and saw Mikey standing there with Tariq close behind her.

"Hey, man," Tariq added.

"How are you?" Beth asked.

"I'm all right, thank you," Mikey warmly answered. His anger melting in her presence, as it always did. He found it almost impossible to stay mad when in her company.

"What happened yesterday?" she asked.

"Nothing much. Just bullshit." Mikey dully replied. Wanting to keep his counsel about the events of the previous day.

"Has Liang been giving you shit?" Tariq asked. "Listen, I've heard the way he talks to you sometimes," he added.

"No more than usual," Mikey lied. He had decided that he didn't want Tariq fighting his battles. He wanted to deal with it himself.

"Please don't shut yourself off to us. We're your friends and we want to help," Beth pleaded.

"I thank you," Mikey smiled. "But I'm okay. I don't need help with them. I can deal with it."

Tariq was about to respond when Beth cut him off. "Ok. Just know that we care. And we're your friends. True friends. We are here for you, whenever you need us." She stroked his arm, before leaving the room. Beckoning Tariq to follow her. When they reached the front counter, she asserted. "This needs dealing with."

"I know," Tariq agreed. "Where's Sean today?" he asked.

"At some meeting," Beth told him. "He seems to be going to a lot of them recently. Do you think everything is okay with the business?" she asked.

"I don't know." Tariq sighed. "I don't think we need to worry about that too much. It's Mikey we need to focus on. You will be finishing your degree in a couple of months and, you already have an offer for a placing. So, you will be moving on soon enough. Leaving Mikey behind with the current state of affairs, is what concerns me," he told her.

"I will be leaving you behind as well. I know you're a lot more equipped to deal with those two snakes than he is. But you both still worry me," Beth informed him.

"You're one of the most genuinely kind and caring souls I've ever come across, Beth. I thank you for all of it. But I will be leaving soon as well," he announced. "Alicia's uncle has a gym on the other side of town. He has offered me a job there, while I study to become a personal trainer."

"That's fantastic news," Beth beamed.

"It was Mikey who gave me the motivation to do it," he informed her. "He made me realise that I am good enough to make something of my life. I'm going to fix this problem for him. Even if it's the last thing I do, before leaving."

"I don't doubt that Tariq," Beth confirmed. "I just don't want you doing something stupid and getting yourself into trouble. Promise me you won't lose your temper. Those two aren't worth it."

"I promise you, I won't," Tariq assured her. "I'm smarter than they are. I will deal with Liang in private. He won't be singing any songs to anybody about it, you have my word on that."

"Ok," Beth nodded. They both quietened upon seeing Rachel and Liang enter. "All right, part timer?" Rachel greeted Mikey. Playfully ruffling his hair.

"Morning," he replied. Feeling annoyed with the invasion

of his personal space though not letting it show outwardly. In the past, he would have been grateful for that sort of interaction with Rachel. But not anymore.

"Is everything okay?" she asked him with concern written all over her face. "Sean said you had to leave yesterday, to deal with some personal issues. I just want you to know, that I'm here for you. If you need me."

"Fuck off! You manipulative parasite," he said in his head. Then spoke out loud, "Thank you, Rachel. But I'm okay."

"All right," she replied. "Just know that I'm here, if you want to talk."

Mikey just nodded and thought. "Never in a million years, will you be lucky enough to get inside my head again."

The day passed quietly, and Mikey didn't speak much. He was polite when spoken to but didn't engage anybody in conversation. He texted Colin in the afternoon, asking if he fancied a beer later. Colin replied in the affirmative and they arranged to meet in the Knowsley. Agreeing to go halves on some goodies.

Mikey made his way there after closing the shop with Tariq. Reassuring him once again, that he was okay.

He found Colin sitting in his usual spot near the pool table. He had company with him. There was another man sitting at his table. Mikey recognised him from the last time he was in there. He had sung along to Mikey's song. Mikey got himself a drink and made his way over.

"Here's the tits and beer lad!" The bald-headed man, who Mikey recognised, exclaimed upon seeing him. "I love that song," he complimented. Embracing Mikey.

Mikey could smell the alcohol on his breath and judged that he must have in the establishment for some time before he had arrived. "Cheers, mate." He smiled back.

"I'm Ian," he introduced himself.

"Mikey."

"Good to meet you again. Let's get shit faced," Ian declared.

"Yeah. Let's get the party started," Mikey agreed.

They chatted and drank for a while. Mainly discussing football and women. Colin handed Mikey his bag of goodies and he went to the toilets to crack it open. Mikey ignored two phone calls from Mr Jefferson and also, one from Tanya. He was having too good of a time, to let anything get in the way of it. He would deal with both of them tomorrow. During a quiet moment of reflection, with Colin and Ian having a debate about football. He realised just how rude he had been to Tom. He would have to apologise to him. But not tonight. Tonight, was about getting off his face with his mates and forgetting about all his troubles.

The beer and powder flowed all night. With the conversation becoming less and less gentlemanly, the more they drank and sniffed. Mikey was even joining in and laughing at the crude remarks made. There was a few renditions of the tits and beer song. With things getting a little too rowdy for the barmaid's liking. Who asked them to quieten down. To which Ian told her. "Oh, get a life, you sour mare." Which invoked laughter from his companions.

This prompted the landlord to come over to their table. Warning them that if they didn't keep a lid on things. He would have to ask them to leave. They promised to behave themselves. Which they did so for the remainder of the evening. Not for any fear of the ageing proprietor. More that they wanted to continue enjoying their beer.

They left just after half past ten. In order to get to Tesco before they stopped serving alcohol at eleven. Mikey had invited them both back to his flat for a drink. They made it there without incident and ordered themselves some more goodies.

Ian stayed until four a.m., before getting a taxi home. Mikey and Colin decided to continue drinking. They drank, sniffed, listened to music, and talked all night. Totally losing track of the time. Before they knew it, the clock had struck seven a.m.

When Mikey realised this. He laughed. "Shit! We best get to bed. Need to get to work."

"Bloody hell," Colin chimed. "Good job I've got the day off."

"Lucky you," Mikey sarcastically said. "I will be lucky to get ten minutes sleep before I need to be up." He knew phoning in sick was not an option. He thought, "Work's sure going to be fun."

Chapter 23

"Well, that was a glorious ten minutes." Mikey laughed out loud. As he crawled out of bed, to get ready for work. His mind was still flying from his drug and alcohol intake. He was floating up in the clouds. He made his bed and set his clothes out for the day. Those good habits now automatic. Even in his delirious state. He showered and stepped out into the street. The was no Tom lurking around this morning. "Small mercies, he thought.

"I am not the insecure one," he told himself whilst walking up the Rock. "Everybody else is. They're literally petrified of each other. That's why they play their games.

They're desperate to keep their position and will hold back anybody they see as a threat. They're sad. I feel sorry for them."

He started to quietly sing the further he walked. Getting a few looks from people passing by. He didn't care and just smiled at them. He was singing 'Minority' by Green Day.

"I wanna be the minority.

I don't need your authority Down with the moral majority 'Cause I wanna be the minority."

"They've sent the fucking army." He laughed to himself. When his eyes fell upon the open shop and saw that Beth, Tariq and Tom were stood waiting inside.

Unbeknownst to him, both Beth and Tariq had decided the previous day, that they needed to involve Mr Jefferson in their plans. Beth had called him and asked to meet. Explaining the premise of what it was about. She got his number from the customer database at Energy Records. Both her and Tariq were aware, that this was a flagrant breach of data protection and would have seen them both dismissed, if it were to backfire on them. They trusted it would not and took the risk. It would prove to be a correct assumption. They met in the Roach Hotel pub, on Rochdale Road. About ten minutes' walk from the town centre, to hatch their plan for the morning. They felt the venue would be safe, as they knew none of their other colleagues frequented the place.

"Get in the kitchen and sort yourself out," Beth ordered him. Upon seeing the state he was in. Mikey opened his mouth to protest, and she instantly cut him off. "Don't you dare. Get out of sight before Sean sees you." She knew their plan would be in tatters if Sean were to see him in such a bleary-eyed state. She knew she had to be harsh, in order to be kind. Being the gentle soul that she is. It was not normal for her to act in this manner. Though, she could bring a raging fire to the surface when it was needed.

Mikey felt an instant pang of guilt and skulked off into the kitchen, without another word. Tariq followed. "Listen, mate," he calmly spoke. "This ends now. I don't want any bullshit. We are here to help you. And we are going to. Whether you like it or not. We're going to speak to Sean this morning and sort it out. That's the bottom line. After today, you won't have to worry anymore. I promise you that. The one favour we need from you is, to look after the front desk while we deal with Sean. Do you think you're up to it?" he asked. Searching his friend's face.

"Yes," Mikey timidly replied. Then hugged Tariq and sobbed a little in his arms. "Thank you," was all he could muster, by way of speech.

Tariq wordlessly held him. He was not entirely comfortable

with this male bonding, but he tried his best to be comforting.

Sean looked agitated as he arrived that morning. It was not without foundation. Two of his employees and his best customer, had all requested his presence as early as possible. None of them had taken no for an answer and he felt obliged to do as he was bid. He knew it would be bad news. How bad? He did not know. He did know that he would find out pretty soon.

"Upstairs, Sean," Mr Jefferson more or less ordered the business owner. They wordlessly ascended the stairs to his office.

"What can I help you with today?" Sean asked. Once they were both seated.

"I need to lay something on the line for you and as a customer, you will listen to me," Mr Jefferson began. Then held his hand up to tell Sean, he was not interested in any response he may have for him. He continued, "I feel a tension whenever I am in your shop. There is an irrefutable atmosphere, being caused by certain employees of yours. Namely, Rachel and your new starter, Liang. You have not seen it, because your ego outweighs your intelligence. I have found them to be rude, incompetent, and plain bone idle. I feel as if I have kept my silence on this for long enough. I wish now that I had said something sooner. But rest assured, I am going to now. I will hold my counsel no longer. I have witnessed verbal psychological abuse, handed out by these two. It is always Mikey who is their target. He is traumatised by it. That young man hasn't got a hurtful bone in his body and what they have put him through, is vile. Your other two employees; Beth and Tariq, feel the same way. I saw them both extremely upset by it yesterday. That is why I am here today. For all three of them.

None of them deserve to be put through what they are being. I know you have been told these things in the past and have done nothing about it. Now, I am telling you again. If you choose not to act this time, there are two options. You are either failing in your duty of care to your employees. Or you are in on it. And that would make it institutional bullying. Either way, it would spell the end for you. I would make damn sure of it. Take that to the bank as a promise. Now, I'm going to let Beth and Tariq come up and tell you how they feel. And you will listen. Goodbye, Sean."

With that, he got up and left the room. He had no interest in anything Sean had to say, by way of reply. A minute later, Beth and Tariq entered the office. Beth sat in the seat opposite Sean. With Tariq standing beside her.

Beth began. Without invitation. "The working conditions here have become completely intolerable."

"I completely agree," Tariq quickly chipped in.

"Furthermore, as I have already told you. The way Rachel and Liang behave towards Mikey, is unacceptable," she continued, "It is nothing short of bullying. We are officially reporting this to you today. We implore you to act. If you do not, we will have no option but to take you to an employment tribunal, to resolve the issue. If it comes to that, we will do so with maximum external publicity. I'm sure that is something you don't want. I have personally witnessed Rachel verbally abuse Mikey and have seen Liang, physically intimidate him. Not only is this unacceptable for him to be subjected to these things. It is also uncomfortable for both of us two, and our customers alike. Who have had to witness some of these exchanges. What we ask of you today is, for you to protect your employee from any further harm. Which in turn will help your business grow in the way you want it to. As this situation, is only hindering that from happening. We want you to extend your duty of care to Mikey, as your employee. Thank you. Now, I believe Tariq would like to express his feelings," she finished with. Looking up at her colleague and friend.

"Firstly, I want to say that I agree with everything Beth has told you today. I will go on record to say that she will have my full support and help, with any further action she deems necessary," he started, "I am going to outline an incident that occurred, which will fully support everything Beth has told you."

He thought for a brief moment about his next words. Then continued, "I was discussing the pros and cons about taking up boxing, with Mikey in the kitchen. When Liang entered, interrupted our conversation and belittled him. Telling him he would never amount to anything physically. He threatened him by saying he would tear him apart if he even thought about it. Then stood over him, with a menacing look on his face. He is much taller than Mikey, so you can imagine how intimidating that must have been for him. That is just one example of his behaviour. There are many others. Which I am happy to share, should I need to do so. At this moment, I feel as if you have enough evidence to go on. Thank you. I hope for a just resolution," he ended with.

Beth instantly stood up at the conclusion of Tariq's evidence and they both left the room.

While the bombshells were being blown up on the first floor, Mr Jefferson asked Liang, "That's a lovely shiner. Have you been fighting?"

"Accident at the gym," he replied not making eye contact and scurrying into the back office.

"You need to learn to be more careful," Mr Jefferson called after him. Then chuckled to himself.

Sean sat alone in his office in stunned silence for a good ten minutes. After the cataclysmic meteors that had rained down upon him that morning. He knew he needed to act. To clear everything up and resolve the situation. His head felt like a tangle of unruly weeds. He was not used to feeling this way. He was normally the one who made others feel that way. He already had the headache of his record label not doing as well as it had. Frantically, himself and Siobhan, had been scouring the local scene for new acts. After their gig at the Deaf Institute, The Protons had informed him that they were splitting up. They could no longer bear working with each other, apparently. They were the main source of income for the label. Always sold the most albums and got the best attendances at gigs. It seemed that gravy train would soon be drying up. If only he could discover another Spark Town. That would set him up until retirement. Alas, there didn't seem to be one lurking anywhere. Now, he had this morning's issue to deal with on top of all that. He decided it best to close the shop for the day and send everybody home. Which he announced to the group when he finally came down.

He told his employees. "I have been made aware of some dangerous electrical issues, that have made it unsafe for us to be open today. They should be resolved by tomorrow. So, come in as normal. Unless you hear otherwise. For today, I need you all to vacate the premises as soon as you're able. I will lock up the shop myself. Have a good day."

With that, everybody collected their belongings and prepared to leave. Beth was already stood outside with Mr Jefferson. She looked him dead in the eye and told him. "You have to tell him, today."

"Tell who what?" he asked. Puzzled.

"You know who and you know what," she replied.

Chapter 24

Mr Jefferson led Mikey down the Rock, back to his apartment. Doing his utmost not to let his nervousness show. His state of anxiety about what needed to be said today, was off the scale. He knew this time was always going to come, sooner or later. He had planned for it. Wanted it. Yearned for it even. Now that time was upon him. All his planned words and actions had seemingly left him. He looked at the young man walking beside him. Seeing the visible signs of a heavy night on the booze. He decided that he must let him rest before any conversation could take place.

When they reached Silver Street, Mikey was about to say his goodbyes to his companion. When Mr Jefferson spoke. "I will come up with you. I want no argument. I insist. You need to get some rest."

Mikey did not protest, and they made their way upstairs. He looked at the old man, in a bit of a daze. Almost searching for instruction. Sensing this, Mr Jefferson quietly told him, "Get yourself to bed. I will be here when you wake up."

Without another word, Mikey went into his bedroom and got into his bed. His mind still whirled with thoughts. Until sleep fell upon him half an hour later.

Mr Jefferson made himself a coffee and sat upon the couch. Switching on the television at a low volume. He flicked through the various channels and settled upon watching the Snooker World Championships. He had always been a fan of the sport and was a keen player in his younger days. He always kept himself abreast of the results and watched it whenever he could. He couldn't keep his mind concentrated on the proceedings, however. It kept wandering back to how he was going to approach the situation at hand. It weighed heavy on him. In truth, it had since he came to this town and first set eyes on Mikey. He needed a release from it all. To begin a new chapter and finally close the old one, for good. The words Beth had spoken to him earlier, were still ringing in his ears. How could she possibly know?

There was no way. He was the only one who knew and nobody else. He hadn't told anybody. That he was certain of. Did she just sense it, by the way he had been acting? Perhaps. After all, she is very perceptive. He would have to speak with her and find out. For now, the time of reckoning was at hand. How would it play out? How would Mikey react? He did not know the answers to those questions. It was not in his hands. All he could do was flip his coin, call heads and hope it landed that way.

The hours passed and he became more worried as time went on. The door buzzer lifted him from his trance. He looked at the clock on the wall and realised it was past five. The hours had flown by. He thought about ignoring it. Then concluded, he best see who it was and get rid of them. As they would probably come back later otherwise. If it was Colin from across the way, he would just tell him Mikey wasn't home. It was not Colin. It was Tanya. He thought quickly and decided to buzz her in. If her and Mikey were going to form a lasting relationship, then she needed to hear this too. So, she may as well hear it now.

He let her into the flat and motioned her to keep her voice down. Explaining that Mikey was sleeping. She told him that she had come over, as she was worried about Mikey. He had not been answering her calls and texts. She wanted to know that he was all right. Mr Jefferson assured her that he was and to take it easy on him. As he had been under a lot of stress lately and wouldn't have been ignoring her on purpose. He showed her an empty bag of cocaine, that he had come across earlier in the day. They both agreed that they needed to say something to him about this. In a tactile way, that wouldn't make him shut himself off.

He told her that he was going to tell Mikey something when he woke up. That was of the utmost importance and would affect his whole future, and hers alike. Should they want to make a go of a relationship together. Tanya told him that after their last date, she had decided that was something she wanted very much. He had been so sweet and caring. He had made her realise that he was somebody, she wanted to form a lasting bond with. Doubts had crossed her mind since then, however. Given the way he had been ignoring her. Her coming here today, was to ascertain whether those fears had any value? What she had learnt this afternoon, made her realise that he needed her help. Not to be instead confronted by her, regarding his behaviour.

There was a palpable tension in the both of them, as they heard Mikey stirring.

He came into the living room and the surprise of seeing Tanya, was plain to see. She immediately rose and gave him a tight hug and kiss. Telling him there was no need to explain himself and they should move on from it. She did, however, caution him that he needed to learn from the experience. Going forward, he would need to be better in his communication. He accepted this and apologised.

"Mikey, can you sit down please?" Mr Jefferson beckoned. "I need to talk to you."

Mikey did sit and began to talk. "I want you to tell me why you're so interested in me? It's been playing on my mind for ages.

You're always hovering around."

"I've been trying to help you." Mr Jefferson explained.

"I'm thankful for that. But, I have a nagging feeling there's more to it than that." Mikey spoke firmly.

"I don't know how to explain it to you."

"Try."

"I can't find the words to say it to you, I'm sorry." Mr Jefferson was getting emotional. "What the fuck is it?" Mikey shouted at the old man.

"I, I... It's all so hard to explain." Mr Jefferson was now stumbling all over himself. He had not felt like this in years. He had learned to control himself years ago and now, all the bad times were coming back to him.

"Is it? You've been following me around like a lost puppy. Don't you think it's a bit sick. You're twice my age. Do you get a kick out of my grief? You sick old bastard!"

"Mikey! Stop it!" Tanya flew in. "Tom has something very important to tell you and you need to listen. Don't you dare be so rude to him. I won't have it. Do you hear me?"

"Yes," Mikey mumbled. Looking down at the floor. Feeling ashamed. "I'm sorry," was his barely audible apology.

"Apologise to Tom, not me," she told him. "It's not my forgiveness you need."

"I'm sorry, Tom. I shouldn't have spoken to you like that." He apologised. "My head is a bit all over the place at the moment. I want to hear what you have to say."

"That's okay," Mr Jefferson soothed. Starting to compose himself more. "I'm the same as you. I told you that we're more similar than you think. I had exactly the same communication and social issues that you experience when I was in my youth. I have helped you because I know how to overcome them. Because

208

I've experienced them. There's a hell of a lot more to tell. Firstly, I have to tell you. My name is not Tom. My name is Mikey Jefferson. We share the same first name. The reason we share the same name, is because you're my son."

Chapter 25

The room was stunned to silence. And stayed that way for over two minutes. Mikey eventually rose. All the years of pent-up anger and rage. All the slights, the bullying, the name calling and praying that he could be normal. All came out of him in those moments. He directed all of this at one person. His newly acclaimed father sitting on his couch. Mikey grabbed him by the throat and threw him to the ground.

"Mikey! No!" Tanya shrieked.

Mikey paid no mind. The toil, angst, and most of all the bad thing. Came out of him as he smashed his fists into the old man. Pounding him, harder with each blow.

Firstly, to the stomach and then pounded his face. All the while, yelling at him. "It's all your fault! All your fucking fault! You abandoned me! You left me to fend for myself! Left me to be brought up by an arsehole, who abused me every day of my childhood! Made my life a living hell! You're the reason I'm not normal and have never fitted in! Everywhere I've gone, I've been the outsider! Nobody has ever cared about me! It's all your fault! Every day in my childhood, I prayed that you would come back and rescue me. Take me away from my living hell. Keep me safe and make me normal. But you didn't. You were too busy having a good fucking time! I just want to be normal! I just want a normal life!"

He raised his fist directly in front of Mr Jefferson's face. Prepared to bring it down full force, on his nose. When Mr

Jefferson suddenly burst out. "I didn't know! I didn't know! I promise you! I promise with every shred of honour I have. I didn't know. I only found out you existed last year!" Mikey shrank back a bit at this.

"Mikey! Please! Stop!" Tanya pleaded. Grabbing hold of Mikey's cocked and loaded right arm. He sank back onto the couch and cried in her arms at this touch.

"That's why I moved here," Mr Jefferson continued. Wiping the blood from his face. "I want to tell you the whole story. Just please, don't hit me anymore. I'm not here to hurt you. I'm here to help you and put things right. I promise upon all promises, that I didn't know about any of this. Until I found out last year."

The room was silent again. Mr Jefferson got himself up to a sitting position. Looked directly at Mikey and began to talk. "Do you remember when I told you about the affair that I had?" he asked.

Mikey nodded and did not speak.

"That was with your mother," Mr Jefferson continued. "I'm ashamed to admit it. Like I've already told you. We had an affair and Nigel found out. That's who your mother was with. I've already told you about the part of him finding out and what happened. What I didn't tell you in the pub, was that it was your mother and she was pregnant.

With you. That's how Nigel found out. He had issues with his ability to produce a child. Some medical term I'm not familiar with. So, he knew the child couldn't possibly be his. I didn't know. I didn't even know she was pregnant. All I knew at the time was, that he found out about the affair and went ballistic. Then what happened, happened. Your mother was sent to prison for unintentional manslaughter. Which is why she had to give you up for adoption. Your mother and me never spoke again after that.

I tried, but she wasn't interested. Blamed me for how her life turned out. I deserve that blame and I carry it round with me every day. I have to tell you, that your mother is unfortunately no longer with us. I was informed by a solicitor that she had taken a drug overdose and passed away. That's when I found out about you.

They told me that she had written into her will, that I was the real father of her child and to only contact me upon her death. Which they did. I can show you everything to prove what I am saying is the truth. That's why I moved here and sought you out. Given the name we both share, you weren't that difficult to trace. I told you the honest truth, when I said I wanted to try and make things right for you, the best I can. I don't deserve forgiveness. It goes beyond that. I just want you to give me a chance to fix you, the best I can. I love you. You are loved and always will be.

Because I love you. I love you. Your mother loved you. She just had demons that she couldn't fix. Because of what we did, all those years ago. Please, please give me a chance to be a part of your life. Just because the first part of your life has been sad, doesn't mean the future can't be bright. I love you and I want to heal you. As best as I can. I love you, son." He wept uncontrollably and was unable to speak any longer.

Silence enveloped the room once again. The sound of the three of them sobbing, was all that could be heard. Mikey finally looked at the man, who was claiming to be his father and croaked. "I'm sorry I hit you. When I first heard your story in the pub, I told you that you were young and would have had no idea how it could have ended up. I stand by that. It's hard, but I stand by it. You have already helped me. You have made me stronger than I ever thought I could be. I just want a normal life. I want a family around me. If you're my family, that means you. Help me,

212

please."

"You never have to apologise to me, ever," Mr Jefferson softly told him. "I am your father and I love you."

Mikey was speechless for a good few moments. Before looking up and asking. "I want to know what you meant about your childhood?"

"I was abused, just like you," Mr Jefferson immediately told him. "With me, it was my stepdad. He had a problem with alcohol and would come home drunk. Abuse both my mother and me. Verbally and physically. I am an only child and my father died when I was young. The trauma of that abuse, stayed with me. It has never left me. But I've learnt to control it. Just like I have been teaching you to do. Learning to have an orderly routine, is key to keeping the monster at bay. So is having people around you, that love you. I swore to myself, that if I ever had children. Things would be different. That I would not allow anything like that happen to them. I failed in that respect. It did happen. It happened to you. I failed you. I would give anything to take that pain away from you. But I can't. I can only help you deal with it, the best you can. So, what we have to do now, is break the cycle. We need to make sure it never and I mean never, happens to your children."

They embraced each other, hard. Mr Jefferson motioned for Tanya to join them, and she did so. All three of them held each other and cried. They cried like none of them had before. All the cards were on the table. There were none left in the pack. A family unit, in the most infant form. Loving and consoling one another.

The hours passed by again. Mikey began to ask questions about his mother. Mr Jefferson did not hold back in answering. He told her that her name was Rita, and she was a fine young lady in her youth. That she had dark hair, just like him. She was very loving and outgoing. Always the life and soul of the party. He spoke of how he and Nigel were friends and that's how he met his mother. They became close and took things a step further than they should have. He said how he deeply regretted not telling her to leave Nigel before they did anything behind his back. She had hinted at as much. Though, he did not heed her. It went without saying, that now that was one of his deepest regrets. There were more tears shed by all, as the night wore on. Mr Jefferson reiterated everything he told Mikey. In terms of wanting to make sure his future could be bright. Nobody had fully taken on board the enormity of what had been spoken about that evening. It would most certainly take a while to sink in. If ever. For now, they had to make the best of what they had and plot a way forward. Which was best for all concerned.

Tanya played her part, by telling the both of them that. "It will be hard work to build your relationship. But, if both parties were willing. Then there is no reason why you can't. Be strong for each other and you can make it work," she implored them.

It was the small hours of the morning when the group turned in to sleep. Mikey and Tanya went to the bedroom and Mr Jefferson, took the couch. The three of them embraced for a long time, before departing to bed.

Chapter 26

Sean pounded into Energy Records the following morning. He had a renewed confidence and vigour about him. Yesterday had caught him off guard. Today he was prepared. He had decided the previous evening, how he was going to deal with the situation. The most straight forward thing was to call Liang. To tell him that he didn't feel as though things were working out and he was ending his employment. He wouldn't have to concern himself with him today. That was the easy part. As Liang had not been with him that long. Under employment law, he could terminate him without much fuss. It had become apparent that he had been causing friction. So "Fuck him," Is what Sean told himself.

Now came the difficult part. He needed to take back control of his workplace. He had always been right about things, and this was no different. All he was interested in, was his business surviving and growing. What he had planned today, had to be done. In order to make that happen. A major restructure now had to take place. All the ducks needed to be lined up. He sat in his office and heard footsteps on the stairs, he knew who it would be.

"Good morning, Siobhan. Please take a seat," he greeted his store manager.

"Morning, Sean," she reciprocated taking the seat offered. "I may have some exciting news regarding new talent." Siobhan smiled to her boss.

"I will be delighted to hear about it, in due course," Sean

informed her. "Right now, we need to have a discussion along a different topic."

"Ok. What can I help you with?" she asked.

"You have been by my side for over fifteen years," he reminded her. "You started on the market stall with me before we managed to get this shop. Those were fun days," he reminisced.

"They certainly were fabulous," Siobhan agreed.

"You have helped this business grow to what it is now and became my store manager along the way. I thank you for all of it," Sean warmly complimented. "Now, I need your help in a different way," he continued.

"By all means. I am willing to do anything to help you. You should know that by now." She smiled at him.

"Good. What I want you to do, is help Mikey," he told her, "I want you to teach him everything you know about your management role. Take him under your wing and groom him for succession."

"Mikey?" she incredulously questioned. "Surely, Rachel is better suited?"

"I have other plans for Rachel," he shot back. With a hint of irritation.

"Why now?" Siobhan asked. "Surely even somebody as incompetent and lazy as him, doesn't need years of training before I retire. In order to do the job properly."

"He's not the incompetent one, you are," he flatly told her.

Siobhan gasped. Though did not speak.

"And it will not be years," Sean continued, "It will be six months before you take early retirement. If you do as I ask and leave quietly. I will grant you the full pension benefits I promised you all those years ago. If you do not, then I will make life extremely difficult for you and, future employment will be hard to come by for somebody your age."

Siobhan was astounded. She stared at the man she had invested fifteen years of her life into. Who now, had just cast her aside, like an unwanted child's toy. She tried to muster up something to say back. Anything. But no words came forth.

Sensing there was no response forthcoming. Sean carried on. "The way I see it is, you have failed to spot the goings on in this business over the last year or so. Your standards have slipped. You have become egotistical and weak. Your performance has been to the detriment of our growth. It is time you were replaced. I am grateful for everything you have done for me, but everything has its endgame. I will work out the exact details of the succession plan and inform you when everything is in place. Once again, I express to you my thanks and gratitude. We have had an amazing ride together. Let's not end it in a crash and get off safely. Now, please have a good day." He smiled and rose from his seat. Nodding towards the door.

Siobhan had gone ghostly white. She was dumbfounded as she made the short walk to her own office.

Sean re-seated himself, took a deep breath and thought. "That's round one complete." He sat in his chair, with a grin on his face. Preparing himself for round two.

He couldn't get his head around how Rachel thought she could get away with pulling the wool over his eyes. He was always going to find her out, sooner or later. He was far too clever not to. Upon analysing her work data, the previous evening. He had found lots of gaping holes. He wondered what possessed her to have the audacity, to think that he would never catch on? He had access to everybody's data, whenever he chose to look. Now he had done so. He knew she had been playing games. Now it was time to find out, exactly what she had to say about that.

"Morning, Rachel. Please take a seat," Sean greeted and instructed his employee.

"Good morning, Sean and thank you very much." Rachel smiled back to him. With a playful toss of her hair.

"I have been looking at some data," he informed her. "I recall you telling me about Mikey being a little lazy and work shy. That's the reason I have done so."

"Good," Rachel commended. "Now you will see exactly what I mean. I always have to pick up the extra workload, for him being bone idle. I don't mind though. You're a wonderful boss," she preened.

"That's not what this tells me," Sean spoke without emotion. In a matter-of-fact way.

"I don't understand," Rachel looked confused.

Sean put a piece of paper in front of her, from across the desk. It was a printout of orders received and who had processed them. All of them time and date stamped. Then told her. "There seems to be big gaps in the orders you deal with. The data doesn't lie. It can't. It has no understanding of the concept. It appears that Mikey has been processing nearly twice as many orders as you. I went back almost six months, and it was more or less the same. Do you care to explain?"

"There must be some sort of mistake," Rachel tried.

"Mistake? How so?" Sean probed and leant back in his chair.

"There must be some of my data missing. I work hard for you. I'm your best worker. I want to go far in my career," Rachel tried to explain.

"Save the performance," he cut her off. "What has been happening is the following: you have quite simply been conning Siobhan and she has fallen for it. I have put my trust in you, and you have betrayed it. You tried to make yourself look good at the expense of your colleague. You manipulated Siobhan and are trying to do the same with me. What you have failed to realise, is that I'm a lot smarter. I have been on to you for ages. I've been biding my time and waiting for the right time to strike. Now the cat is out of the bag. You are making my business underperform and I won't allow that. I have been left with no other option, but to dismiss you today. For gross misconduct. You have the right to appeal. Should you choose to do so. But be aware, my lawyers will eat you for breakfast if you do. I will allow you the opportunity to say goodbye to your colleagues before you leave. Good luck in the future."

"My daddy will hear of this," Rachel sobbed. "You can't treat me this way."

"I can and I have. Now, please leave my office," Sean ordered her.

Rachel wiped the tears from her eyes and left the room. Annoyed by what had just happened. She thought about how she could get herself out of this.

She made her way downstairs, to the back office. Ignoring Tariq on the way and with Beth listening to an insistent customer, her progress was not halted. There was only one person she needed to speak to. Mikey was her friend. He could resolve this nonsense for her. After all, she had always been kind to him and helped him when nobody else would.

"Hi, Mikey," she smiled to him. With a stroke of his shoulder, with him sitting at his desk.

"Good morning," was his polite, though somewhat flat reply.

"I want to apologise for any misunderstandings there may have been, about my behaviour towards you," she delicately spoke to him.

"I'm listening," Mikey told her.

"Sean has got this crazy idea in his head. That it would be best if I were to leave," she began. "He has left it up to me, though he thinks it best if I do. Because he thinks there is a problem with the way I treat you. I have always had a special love in my heart for you. I feel you're special to me. I want the best for you. I love all my colleagues here, especially you. I adore my work here and want it to continue. I have always helped you in every way I can. I apologise if I have ever come across as short tempered or off. I just have a lot of stress at the moment. I'm moving apartments and I'm having boy troubles. I just want to move on from this." She finished and looked shyly at her colleague.

"Are you aware that in that so called apology, you used the terms, I, I'm, me, my or others similar; a total of twenty times?" Mikey asked.

"Sorry?"

"At what point; before Sean spoke to you this morning, were you going to come and apologise to me?"

"I, I'm not sure."

"The truth is you weren't." Mikey spelled out for her. "Which means you're not sorry for your behaviour. You're horrified that you've been called out for it. You're saying these things to me, to try and save your own skin. Because all you're interested in, is yourself. Your wants your needs, that's all. I do forgive you for your actions and behaviour. I have to tell you that. I have done so because you have never been taught to be better. Therefore, you maybe don't understand that it is wrong.

Forgiveness is closure for both of us. I want you to learn from this. That is the best thing that can come out of this situation. You need to analyse and understand your behaviour. Work out where and how you went wrong. Don't beat yourself up about it. Just make sure you don't repeat it. Make yourself better for the future. Grow as a person and get better. I don't want to continue our working relationship. That being said, I genuinely wish you the best for the future. I want you to be happy in yourself and the people you choose to surround yourself with. Be grateful for everything you have and build a happy future. My heart goes out to you. There is too much pain in this world, for me to feel any other way," he concluded. Then thought to himself. "Wow. How did I make a speech like that? I never thought I would be capable. Fear should be an accelerator, not a brake," he concluded to himself.

Rachel looked helpless, standing in the middle of the room. Mikey rose from his desk, gave her a tight hug, and parted with. "Go well, Rachel. There is goodness inside you. Please let it shine."

Rachel held on to him for some time. Before silently departing Energy Records for the last time. There would be no appeal regarding her dismissal.

Chapter 27

Morning rolled over to afternoon and Sean was in his office. Preparing to have his meeting with Mikey. It would be the final piece in his jigsaw. He decided there would be no need to talk with either Beth, or Tariq. Beth would be leaving soon enough once she had finished her degree. Which he had no doubt she would get the grade needed to earn the placement she had been offered. As far as Tariq was concerned, he knew he could control him and bring him back into line. Once Beth was no longer there to plant seeds of mischief in his mind. Which he knew was the cause of his unruliness of late. Sean was always right and the plan he had concocted, had one more act to fulfil. Mikey would be happy enough with his forthcoming promotion and be grateful to him for it. That would make him bow to his every whim, just like Siobhan had done for so many years. After today's business had been taken care of, he needed to begin the process of recruiting a couple of new staff members. To replace Rachel and Liang in the back office. One needed to be hired immediately.

The other in a few months' time. Mikey could remain there while he trained the first of the new staff members. Then begin his work with Siobhan afterwards. Leaving the one already trained by him, to do the same with the second new starter. Having three full time staff members in the back, was one of Siobhan's stupid ideas and it was not needed. It cost the company too much in wages. Beth's replacement could be put on hold for now. He sat back and grinned, extremely satisfied with himself.

As he prepared to call Mikey up.

After Rachel had departed and the dust settled on that. With the shop being quiet, Mikey approached the front desk, where his remaining colleagues were. Telling them he needed to enlighten them with some news. He proceeded to tell them how he had found out the previous evening, that Mr Jefferson was indeed, his father. Beth immediately asked him how he felt about that? And Mikey told her how he reacted initially. The fact that after hearing the full story, he was now ashamed of his actions. To which Tariq joked. "Maybe you don't need that boxing training, after all?"

This invoked laughter from the three of them. He then told them how they had talked along with Tanya, into the small hours the previous evening. About their plans for the future. His two colleagues were excited by what he told them and offered their support in any way he needed it. He thanked them and asked if they would consider getting involved? Considering what they had planned for their own futures. The both of them agreed it was a project, that they would very much like to be a part of. They decided to work out the details at a later date. The phone in the back office then began to ring. It was Sean, inviting Mikey up to his office.

Tariq spoke when he came back into the room. "I will be going up there myself later." "What for? May I ask?" Mikey politely enquired.

"Going to hand my notice in," Tariq told him. "I'm going to start at the gym and begin my training next week."

A beaming smile came across Mikey's face. "I'm absolutely made up for you. It's just the beginning for you, mate."

"Cheers, mate," Tariq enthused. "I just hope I'm going to be good enough," he lamented.

"You're more than good enough. You will boss it like you do

the boxing ring," Mikey encouraged.

Tariq had a grin from ear to ear and they fist bumped. Before Beth cautioned Mikey. "Don't let him coerce you. Stick to your guns."

Mikey just nodded and began the climb up to Sean's office.

"Good afternoon, Mikey. Please sit down." Sean politely invited him.

Mikey wordlessly sat down. He decided words were not necessary at this point.

"I wanted to follow on from what you told me the other morning. About wanting to prove your worth as an employee," Sean told him.

Mikey just nodded. So, Sean continued. "I have been going through some data and it seems Siobhan has been misreading the situation. It appears that she has been wrong to accuse you of the things she has. I want to firstly apologise on her behalf, for the mistake she labelled as yours. After doing my due diligence on the issue, I have found conclusively, that it was Rachel who processed that order, not you. You have my sincerest apology for her tardiness. You have been a valued employee of mine since the moment you walked through the door. I have always believed in you and knew you had the potential to go far…"

Mikey had heard just about enough. He interrupted by asking, "So, why did you tell me I needed to buck my ideas up?"

Sean was a little shocked by the question. He took a moment to think and replied. "Only because of the feedback I was getting from Siobhan."

"Do you know how much that hurt me?"

"I'm sure it was painful and now I want to make it right."

"Did you not think to make your own enquiries? Especially after both Beth and I, were adamant that it wasn't me? How about when I told you that I was being psychologically bullied? You mocked me."

"I see now that I was mistaken."

"Mistaken? If an employee comes to you with something as serious as that, you should at the very least, investigate it. Don't you think?"

"I have and that is why Rachel and Liang are no longer with us."

"You failed me. You threw me out to the wolves, and it nearly destroyed me."

"I apologise. Now I am going to put it right."

"How can you possibly do that?"

"I am going to give you a chance to advance your career," Sean grinned whilst announcing.

Mikey thought about responding. Then thought it better to hear him out, before revealing his hand.

"I want to promote you to store manager," Sean revelled in telling him. "Siobhan has decided to take early retirement in six months. She is going to take you under her wing during the time she has left. Teach you everything she knows, so you will be ready when the time comes."

"Siobhan," Mikey thought. "There really is nothing more irritating than a fool with a big mouth. It appears the less intelligence a person has, the bigger their mouth.

Making up for one shortcoming with something else. Should I judge somebody's intellect by their vocal level?" he asked himself.

Then came back into the room and asked. "Why would I want to spend another second in Siobhan's company?"

"Because she is the manager here and can teach you everything she knows," Sean told him.

"You see, Sean." Mikey began. "Since I've started to cut out the dickheads from my diet, my life has been so much healthier. I will be turning this promotion down. I sat down with my father and my girlfriend last night and we decided that we would be better served going to into business for ourselves."

"I thought you didn't know who your father was?" Sean asked.

"I didn't. Until recently. You know him very well, though." Mikey grinned.

Sean looked a little dumbfounded. Something Mikey had never seen before. So, he pressed on and announced. "Mr Jefferson is my father. That's why he's been frequenting the shop so much. Not because of your business savvy or fantastic product range. He's been coming to see me."

Sean was stunned to silence with that bombshell. He finally found his voice to ask. "What type of business are you thinking of setting up?"

"It won't any type of business you will be familiar with." Mikey spoke with confidence. "It's going to be a not-for-profit charity. To help people. We are going to make the community as a whole, better. It will be a place where people can come and talk about their problems. A help centre. For people struggling. We want to pick people up, not grind them down. Like most try to. We know that our concept is a minority way of thinking. But we believe there is enough good out there to make it work. One part of the business will be a café, where all your food and drink are free. As long as you agree to partake in community projects to help others, after you have received it yourself. Everybody has to give back once they have received. The other aspect is where my wonderful girlfriend; Tanya, comes into play. She will be sourcing an allotment, where we can grow our own food and give out weekly food parcels to underprivileged families in the community. Where we will also offer weekend jobs to the children of these said families, to give them confidence and valuable work experience. My childhood may have been a right off. But now, we can help to break that cycle and look after our next generation, better. I would like to offer you the opportunity to volunteer your services for this project. To help in any way you can."

"It will never work," Sean flatly told him.

"Oh, it will." Mikey contested.

"And what are you going to call this project of yours?" Sean sneered.

"The Underdogs. Seems appropriate," Mikey informed him. "You don't need to be concerned about me leaving you short staffed. I will continue to work here, until an appropriate replacement can be found."

Sean gave a defiant grin, before telling him to leave his office.

Mr Jefferson was downstairs when Mikey reappeared. He was deep in conversation with Beth and Tariq was dealing with a customer, so he waltzed to his desk in the back office. "Alone. Just like old times," he thought.

"How did you know?" Mr Jefferson was asking Beth.

"I've been convinced for a while," she revealed. "You have always made a thing about making sure he was all right and tried your best to communicate whenever you saw him."

"Was I that obvious?" Mr Jefferson asked. Chuckling.

"A little bit." Beth giggled back. "Plus, the fact that you both have the same jaw line and some of your mannerisms are the same."

"There really is no way of hiding anything from you, is

there?" he complimented.

"I would hope you wouldn't try," she teased.

"So, Tariq has decided to stay on until you graduate?" Mr Jefferson asked.

"Yeah, he's been protective. Bless him," Beth warmly answered. "Decided that he doesn't want to leave me alone with Sean and Siobhan, once Mikey leaves. He changed his mind after realising he will be gone soon. He said he will speak to Alicia's uncle and explain. Both of us are excited by your new project and be rest assured, we will help in any way we can."

"I know you will," Mr Jefferson confirmed. "You two are wonderful young people, with bright futures. I especially want to thank you, for all the help you have given to my son."

"You're welcome and he deserves a chance at happiness," Beth concluded.

"You're not wrong there." He agreed.

Sean then walked past the front desk and out of the shop. "Excuse me," Mr Jefferson said to Beth.

"Seany boy," he spoke to his back. Not for the first time.

"Mr Jefferson," Sean coldly responded. Turning to face him. "I'm aware you're having staff issues," Mr Jefferson let on.

"They're not as bad as your face, by the look of it," Sean retorted.

Mr Jefferson ignored that and told him. "Maybe you should learn to treat them better." Before clapping him on the arm and walking off down the Rock, with a spring in his step.

Chapter 28

Mikey did work at Energy Records for the next month. While he trained an able replacement for himself. He sensed the new recruit; Hannah, was a major upgrade on what had gone before. She was hard working and willing to learn. Also, a pleasant person to be around. His newfound father and Tanya worked tirelessly on getting The Underdogs project up and running. His dad poured a lot of his retirement money into it for start-up capital. As they waited for approval on government funding. Which they got in due course, and things began to take shape.

Beth made good on her promise to help out. Once the café was up and running, she used her newly earned psychology degree to full effect. Listening to the people who came in and acting as the charity's de facto counsellor. She found a new hobby in baking cakes whilst being there. After helping Tanya with some, she really enjoyed the process, and would now do it whenever she could. She also found it good therapy for the people she helped, as it gave them an opportunity to talk and open up, whilst baking. She warmed to Tanya very quickly and the two of them had gotten close. Or. "Thick as thieves," as Mikey put it one day. The one thing she didn't share, was Tanya's enthusiasm for the allotment. Having gone there once, that was enough for her to realise, she was not green fingered in the slightest. Before leaving Sean's employment, she had told Reggie the plans for the new project, when he came in to do some work and have round three with Siobhan. He responded to the news by telling her.

"That is a top thing to do. The finest electrician in the land, will volunteer his services to do your electrics."

To which Beth joked, "If you have his number, please forward it on to me."

Reggie laughed and told her, "I will leave you my business card. Call me when you need my finery."

Beth thanked him and they shared a warm smile before he departed.

For Tariq's part, he loved to get. "Down and dirty" at the allotment. That's how he described the process at the place. He found it invigorating and realised he liked to be at one with nature. He also came through on his word. He would take anybody who wanted to go, down to the gym he now worked at. His girlfriend's uncle, having also been true in allowing him to work there while he studied. He would offer any support he could to the people who wanted it. Whether they wanted to just gain a bit of fitness or wanted to build their confidence. He was there for them. If they wanted to do weight training or try a bit of boxing, he showed them the correct structure to follow and encouraged them. He loved his new lifestyle and was grateful for everything he now had. He told his girlfriend as much; and although, he didn't admit any past infidelities to her. He became a much more doting boyfriend and vowed, never to do anything of the sort again. Alicia came herself to check out the place and instantly fell in love with it. She made herself available to make deliveries of the food parcels. As did Mr Jefferson and Beth's boyfriend, Rob. As they were the only three of the group that could drive.

Mikey spent more time getting to know his father and family background. He learned that his name had originated from his father's grandfather's nickname. His wife would always call him

Mikey and the name stuck when they had their first-born son. It had been passed on ever since. His dad surmised that Mikey's mother must still have had feelings for him. Considering she chose that name, for her child. They planned a trip up to Darlington. He was informed that unfortunately, both his paternal grandparents had now passed away. Though, his dad believed that his maternal grandmother at least, was still alive. They agreed to try and make contact over the phone, before appearing on her doorstep. As the best course of action. Mikey knew now, why he had always yearned for home. It was because he never knew where home was. Now he did and he no longer pined for it. It held too many bad memories for his father and himself. Given the knowledge he now had. He realised that the past, belonged in the past. The bad thing was never going to go away. He knew that. It would be with him until the day he died. He could now control it much better, however. Through the teachings of his father, he had been able to put processes in place, to keep it locked away. The best he could. Mental illness is not something you can eradicate, he realised. You just had to find a way to control it, and not the other way round. That's what The Underdogs project was all about. Giving people who had it tough, a chance to grow and be better. To help them see there is a way out and that they are loved. To teach the mantra of your past does not define your future.

The underprivileged and social misfits, like himself. Can rise and make a good life for themselves. They just needed somebody to show them how. Mikey decided that there should only be two rules at the Underdogs café, or allotment. The first one, every question should be answered openly and honestly. That gave everybody the best possible chance to be helped. Number two, discretion, and confidentiality.

Anything that was said, remains between those people. Unless told otherwise. That went for group discussions, or one on one private conversations. Only the persons involved in a particular conversation, would ever know the contents of it. It had to be that way. He remembered what Beth had told him. "Friendship is built on trust. If we don't have that. We have nothing." He couldn't have put it better himself. So much so, he decided to ask her permission, to use it as the slogan for the whole project.

His relationship had deteriorated with Colin, however. Both his dad and Tanya had expertly talked him into the fact, that drug taking with people who don't care for you. Is a mugs game. He could see that now. But he needed to know if Colin was a true friend. He told him he was no longer interested in that type of thing and wanted to do his best to stay off it. He did say that he hoped they could still go out for a few drinks together, just nothing as involved as they had done so previously. Colin reiterated that he was far too young to be settling down and would regret it in a few months. When he's stuck with a boring girl, who no longer lets him get on it. Mikey told him that he too, should think of settling down and that he may enjoy the warmth of a family. Offered him the chance to come to the café and see how he liked it. If he did, then he could by all means get involved. Colin rebuffed this and told him he was welcome to his sad little life. Mikey told him he would always be there for him, should he change his mind. Colin scoffed at this and closed the door to his apartment. Mikey thought to himself. "Please learn, my friend. Before it's too late."

Chapter 29

As the month's rolled by. Things got up and running properly and the correct amount of funding was in place. It seemed that everything was on track. Mikey and Tanya, along with his dad. Sat in the living room of their newly rented house on Rochdale Road. Tanya had pretty much been living at Mikey's apartment recently. So they decided it best to get a place together. As they were practically falling over each other, in his small one bed apartment. They had plans to buy in the future; but for now, this would suit. Mikey was revelling in telling them about Tommy. Who had been frequenting the café to tackle his demons. He was making fantastic progress and was trying to convince Mikey to put chicken and chips on the menu. Mikey told them. "He's even got a funny song for it. He said the humour will drum up business. It goes like this;"

One forty-nine, one forty-nine Chicken 'n' chips, only one forty-nine. Come to the restaurant.

Have a good time.

Chicken 'n' chips only one forty-nine.

The group burst out into uncontrollable laughter at this. Tanya said to Mikey. After somewhat composing herself. "God. Stop it! It's not only the song. It's the silly little dance you did to go with it." Which invoked more laughter

Tanya declared that it would be nice if they went out for a few drinks to celebrate. Mr Jefferson concurred and said, "Why don't we go back to where it all began for us?

The Old White Lion."

"What a wonderful idea, Tom," Tanya agreed. She had decided to keep calling him Tom. As calling him Mikey as well, would be far too confusing.

To which he had replied, "Hopefully you will call me Dad one day, if the lad plays his cards right." Ruffling his son's hair with affection.

They descended upon the pub half an hour later, in a taxi. Mr Jefferson got the drinks and they talked about various topics for the next ten minutes, before Mikey excused himself to go to the bathroom.

There he encountered a short balding man, who was startled by Mikey's entrance. Mikey knew what he was holding in his hand. The man searched the new occupant of the toilets face for a clue as to his intentions. Then by way of placating the situation, asked, "Do you want one?"

Mikey stared at the snow-white powder on the end of that key, for a long moment. Before politely declining the offer and heading back to his family.

Epilogue

Temptations

The flame that always burns That can't be put into words Sat beneath the diamond sky

Tricks of the mind, tender and sly Say to go without, would bring fright A rapture to craft and bring delight Your friend to the end, always there Or an enemy if you can be aware The pleasures are a temporary flare

The darker the sky, after which they came No matter who it is you blame

The answer is how you play your game.

The End.